Secret Seasons

Secret Seasons

by Kathi Cousineau

Xulon Press

Xulon Press
2301 Lucien Way #415
Maitland, FL 32751
407.339.4217
www.xulonpress.com

Printed in the United States of America.

ISBN-13: 9781545628188

Dedication

This book is dedicated to my husband, Walter. Thank you for your exquisite input, delightful additions and your faith that keeps me whole.

In Memory of Lou Cousineau, 1931 ~ 2012

Acknowledgements

Linda Cole, Lifetime Editor, [Retired]

A special thank you to Ms. Linda Cole, (Mrs. Steven Cole), for her exceptional editing of this book.

Disclaimer

This is a fictional book. The characters and events are derived from the creative imagination of the author. Names, characters, businesses, places, events, locales, and incidents are either the products of the author's imagination or used in a fictitious manner. Any resemblance to actual persons, living or dead, or actual events is purely coincidental.

Kathi Cousineau ~ Author

Table of Contents

Chapter One

Before She Knew God

It was a beautiful spring morning, April 1995, when Shannon and her husband, Jay, arrived in Denver, Colorado. The sky was clear; the sun was shining above the snow-capped peaks of the "Mile High" city. They'd packed all their belongings into her car, not for a vacation, but for a move across country. Shannon believed her husband's talk. He'd convinced her the move would be good for them. He spoke of 'making a fresh start'. She wondered what that meant, since they'd just been married, and that alone, was a 'start' for her. She wanted to believe he'd quit drinking. She wanted to believe even when doubts plagued her. One time, only a few weeks before the wedding, he'd verbally abused her about changing the oil in her car. He'd been drinking. She ignored the warning sign. She felt guilty for not being responsible.

Shannon had worked since she was twelve years old. She started babysitting, doing odd jobs, and saved all her money. She started waitressing at age sixteen and saved that money, too. At age nineteen she wanted nothing more than to leave the tired, little town of Coleville, Ohio.

Her brother, Ken Bradley, had done it! He left for Cleveland right after high school. He began working for a moving company and eventually worked all the way to dispatcher for a major trucking line. He was twenty-three years old when Shannon graduated from High School. Ken loved his work. He loved to be a part of the entire United States. The buzz words of the times were about being 'a mover and a shaker', and Ken was that!

Shannon loathed the thought of staying in Coleville. She watched her friends from high school stay there. They had low-paying jobs with little hope for the future. Very few of them went to college and most of them never thought about it. Shannon wanted to go college but didn't allow herself to think about it. There was no money. She'd finish every thought of college with a sigh, and say, "No way."

Her dad left the family when she was three years old; she hardly knew him. Shannon naturally adopted and absorbed her mom's financial fears. To stay in Coleville, get married, have children, and repeat her mom's life was abhorrent! When Jay wanted her to marry him, and move away, she went for it. In her trusting manner and innocence, she believed she loved him. Marriage was an opportunity, a 'ticket out'.

Jay had some money from selling his car. It wasn't a lot of money, but enough for the trip and an apartment. They drove Shannon's car. She'd saved for the car for years. She paid cash for it.

Jay was a good person when sober. Shannon felt secure during the trip as he didn't drink and seemed not to want to.

Shannon had just turned twenty years old, before they were married, and he was twenty-five. They'd met as employees at the bowling alley, only three months prior. She waitressed on league nights. She liked her job because her employer taught her about payroll deductions. He was always surprised she wanted to know. Shannon wasn't unhappy with her income; she was inquisitive about 'how things work'. Jay bartended at the bowling alley. He pursued her constantly, always joking, and making her laugh.

Shannon's mom, Shelly, liked Jay. He had a job, and that was all her mom needed to know. Shelly was pregnant with Ken, at age sixteen, and married the father. Then she had Shannon at age twenty-one. By age twenty-four, she was a single mom, with little education. She loved her kids and had hope for their lives even through her struggles. She may have had more confidence in her kids than in herself. Life was not easy for her financially. Shelly thought Jay would be security for her daughter and never questioned it. There was no money for a nice wedding. A small one would have to do. Only twelve people were there, all of which were Shannon's family members, and a few of her friends.

The couple had fun together as they ventured along the freeways. They traveled on Highway I40 West to Colorado. Jay made jokes and it was a lively time. He said he had a good job waiting for him in Denver.

Before they left, Shannon's brother, Ken, put a note in her hand. Then he said, "In case you need something." He smiled. It was the phone number of a good friend of his, who grew up with him in Coleville, and now living in Phoenix, Arizona. Ken didn't particularly like Shannon's guy, Jay. He had suspicions about him, but he shoved it aside, not wanting to interfere in his sister's decision. He also doubted his own suspicions. He justified his feelings. Possibly he was being too protective of his sister and mom. Besides, Jay seemed to charm everyone else. Sometimes the two of them would have a short laugh together.

Shannon's grandmother gave her a gift of money at the wedding. She shared some of that gift with her husband, but she didn't share the note Ken gave her. She tucked it away in her wallet.

Arriving early in the day they looked around for an apartment to rent. Denver's University District was great. They found a place and moved in that afternoon. Shannon went busily about unpacking boxes and arranging things. Jay went to find the closest store in the area. She put items away in the bathroom and brushed out her long, shiny hair. She was grateful to her grandmother for the wedding gift, but even more grateful she'd inherited her grandmother's genes!

Shannon, attractive and elegant, at 5'9', 125 lbs., was beautiful beyond her years. Her eyes stretched across her face in a striking, blue-green color. Her long, very dark, brown hair was soft and had a brilliant shine. She was a trusting soul and receptive, but she wasn't stupid.

Shannon emptied the ice chest and prepared to make dinner out of what was left. A thrill grabbed her heart when she looked out the kitchen window of the apartment. She saw the beautiful buildings of the University Campus. They were old, brick buildings, surrounded by trees, columns, and traditional design. She wanted that! She wanted college life and higher education. She could see the names of the buildings. She could see the science and technology buildings. Even though biotechnology, healthcare and computer science were beginning to explode in demand and growth, it wasn't her area of interest. The internet was extremely small then but growing fast. There it was, a College University, and all the information she wanted, sitting right at her grasp.

She remembered going to the elementary school library, on her own, in fourth grade. She searched and searched for something she couldn't find. None of the childhood books satisfied her. She loved to read. She wanted to read something inspirational; something about how to overcome obstacles, how to be rich, how to have success, how to make dreams come true.

Shannon's mom, Shelly, was 'all mom'. She loved her kids and their friends, too. When Shannon's friends came over, she'd get out unsweetened chocolate, milk and sugar, and make a huge pot of hot chocolate for them. Shannon was very popular in school because she loved everyone. She'd bring home friends of all kinds, rich or poor, known or unknown. She was voted for everything the students voted on. She was even voted for positions she didn't run for! Shelly, didn't care much about accomplishments in the work world. Survival, and keeping the kids fed, was all she could do.

Shelly's husband, Ken and Shannon's dad, was a drinker. He drank nightly, but he wasn't a mean-spirited person. He just walked out one day. He said he couldn't be a good husband or father. Shelly managed to raise the kids on practically nothing. She spent her days working and wondering how she'd make enough money for food and rent. She didn't know all the creativity in her daughter's head. She didn't have the freedom to give them all the attention she wanted to.

One time, at a very young age of only five years old, Shannon's music box stopped working. It was a pretty music box that played a lullaby song and the ballerina twirled to the music. She tightened the turnkey underneath to wind it, but it was stuck, and it didn't play or dance anymore. Without a dad to help her, she decided to fix it herself. With the focus of a brilliant child, she turned the music box over. She saw she needed a screw driver to loosen the plate on the bottom. She ran into her brother's room and asked him for one. He was ten years old and busy learning how to set up a ham-radio system in the house. He couldn't wait to connect with people all over the United States! He handed her the screw driver and said, "Bring it back!" Shannon ran back to her room. It seemed to take an hour for her to get the screws turned, one by one, to open the box. Finally, the bottom fell off. She peered inside. "Ohhh, there's a penny stuck in here." Shannon remembered she'd used the music box as a piggy-bank for her coins. With complete attention to the love of the music box, she used her thumb nail to loosen the penny and slide it out of the gears. The ballerina began to twirl, and the song played! With excitement and happiness, she pranced back to Ken's room and returned the screwdriver. Running back to her room, she sat with a smile, listening to the song and watching the ballerina dance. She held the music box lovingly with her little hands.

Dinner was ready when he came home with groceries. She opened the bags and braced herself as she saw the bottle of whiskey. "Oh no," she thought. "This isn't going to be good."

The next day Shannon awoke on the couch in forbidding silence. She hadn't slept much. She shook uncontrollably all night. She got up and stepped quietly into the bathroom. The bruises were ugly along her arms. Some of them could be covered up by shirt sleeves but one was along the upper, hairline of her face. Memory flooded her mind as shock, fear and horrific anger overtook her. He'd drunk the entire bottle of whiskey. At first, he began to stand behind her in a threatening stance. When she turned to look at him he slapped her across the face. When she ducked, he slapped her again. He started in accusing her of things she didn't do.

Then it got worse. He locked the doors and the windows. He began to force her to lie that she did those things. He demanded she speak it, speak out loud, that she did, what he said she did. He forced her to lie many times. Then he began to make her repeat his words back to him in perfect order. When she messed up out of fear, he charged across the room and butted his head into hers, hard! He looked for opportunity to force his rage upon her, so he created conversation she'd naturally have fears about. Then her fear enraged him more.

Over the course of hours of extreme control, he punched her, bruised her ribs, kicked her in the shins and threw her against the wall. He told her he was going to do something to her mom. He told her he was going to put her in the hospital. He told Shannon he was going to cut up her face with a knife.

Shannon imagined herself having a gun in her hand. The next thought was 'no', he'd just push her hand and grab the gun. Any thought of fighting back was wrong. She knew she had to 'take it'. She had to endure it. She kept herself in complete subservience, doing everything he told her to do. She knew only one thing for sure; if she fought back, she'd *die*.

She'd been raised going to church. Her brother, Ken, had a relationship with God. Shannon believed, 'there is a God'. She kept praying inside herself, screaming for help. She prayed over and over, *"God, please help me."*

There was no way out of the apartment.

Shannon prayed quietly, internally, that her life wasn't over.

She glanced quickly at Jay across the room. Her glance was unnoticed. He seemed to be tiring. From moment to moment she didn't know what would happen next. He could be looking tired, or he could be planning something worse.

Then her prayers were answered.

Maybe God and his Angels were trying to get the neighbors to turn off their stereo, so they could hear the distress next door. Maybe God and his Angels were whispering in the ear of a policeman to turn right or left.

Her prayers were answered in the best way for her to hear Him. She remembered a book she'd read. It came to her perfectly clear. It was about angels and their messages to people. It was about a woman who'd faced death. Shannon remembered the woman was told by angels, "in the face of rage, try kindness." As irrational and absurd it seemed, to do such a thing, it was her hope and she didn't hesitate to follow it. She waited for the right moment though, and her opportunity came.

He had a brief pause. He was leaning against the kitchen counter. It was then she spoke softly and kindly to him. She did what the book said to do. She did it, as if it were completely sincere, and she didn't know how she did it. She spoke in a clear, sweet voice; a voice that came out of nowhere! She said, "Oh Jay, I just want to thank you for all the good things you've done for me."

Shannon glanced very quickly at him and then moved her head away. She didn't dare look directly into his eyes. He was looking down and not at her. She thought she saw an effect of her statement on him. She glanced back quickly again and saw his alcoholic induced, insane mind, bouncing between extremes. She was still trapped, and the rage could come back even worse.

The kindness she exhibited had somehow caged him. She could see Jay vacillating in the contradiction of a split mind. He couldn't integrate the two minds. He couldn't integrate the two powerful motives because the extreme was too vast! Shannon could tell he wanted to continue in the rage, but he couldn't do it. He'd lift his head and then it would drop. His head nodded and then it dropped down. She waited. She looked away. Then weakness and exhaustion overcame him. She heard him stumbled to the bedroom and fall into the bed.

Shannon was too afraid to leave. She wasn't sure if he was asleep. She didn't want to make any noise. She waited for morning. She heard him stirring, awakening in the bedroom. There was no time for her to assess anything. It wasn't possible to suppress the pounding emotions inside her. It was completely impossible to stop the pounding outside of her head. It extended in vibrations one or two feet around her upper body.

She knew she could 'fake it'; act as if things were 'OK'. All she could hear were his words, and all she could see was his face shoved into hers, one inch away, forcing his words into her mind, "*I'm going to kill you.*"

She walked from the bathroom to the kitchen. She swept up the broken whiskey bottle off the floor and started coffee. She tried to act 'normal' when he walked in. It was early morning. He acted as if nothing happened; no apologies, no asking her if she was ok; no word or thought of the 'night of horror.'

Moving quietly about the kitchen she acknowledged him as little as possible while he rattled on about taking a drive to see the neighborhood. The sun was just coming up. It seemed strange timing, but she followed him to the car. The sunny, picturesque morning went unnoticed, as Shannon took stock of where they were. She watched all freeway signs, and streets signs in the area. He pulled off the highway and into a near-by park. She walked behind him as he strolled to a picnic table. Shannon's eyes darted, taking in a calculated view of the park, the buildings outside of the park, and distances around her. She didn't look at him, but she heard him drop something on the picnic table. She was sitting sideways to him at the end of the table. Acting casual and unaffected, she stared off at the trees in the distance.

She noticed the restroom building about a hundred feet away. She thought of a possible escape. The women's room was on the front side, facing them, and men's room on the back. Before she could plan an action, he got up and headed to the men's restroom. When she saw him disappear into the entrance, she jumped! He'd left the car keys and his wallet on the table. She didn't think another thought about the wallet. She grabbed the keys, and walked very fast, in the opposite direction of the restrooms. Then she ran! She ran to the edge of the park and entered a border of tall trees and bushes. The parking lot was below her. She slid down a small hill and scrambled to her feet. She saw her car and ran to it. Fumbling with the key, she got in the car. Even though it would take time for him to come out of the restroom, she feared he'd see her. In fact, she feared he was right behind her. Her fear escalated. She locked the door and windows. She jammed the key into the ignition. She felt fear again the car wouldn't start. The engine fired up. She felt he'd be right in front of her blocking the car. She pulled out of the parking lot and onto the road. Glancing into the rearview mirror once, there was no one in sight.

The park road came out along the freeway. She entered the freeway, not knowing where she was going. She only knew the name of her brother's friend, and she knew Phoenix was southwest of Denver. She saw an exit coming up and took it. It said, 'I70 West', and she drove, frantically, miles and miles, and miles, without stopping, until the gas needle was pegged on empty.

The sign said, 'Grand Junction, Colorado." Shannon had driven two hundred and fifty miles south of Denver.

During the drive, there was nothing but urgency to get as far away as she could, but another urgent thought stopped her. "He's going to call my family!" Shannon knew she had to get a grip on things. She pulled into a gas station with a convenience store. Shaking, she bought a bottle of water. She paced outside the store by her car, waiting for the pay phone to be free.

Shannon's brother, Ken, had a very strong intuition regarding his sister. He was a believer in God. He had much more faith in God than his sister or mother then. He had a relationship with God from a young age. Even though the father was a drinker, he'd instilled in Ken, knowledge of belief in God. Shannon was too young to have received it.

Ken's desk at work was loaded with lists of area codes, maps, vendors, and notes pinned everywhere. Software programs were in development and cell phones just becoming universal. Work was harder and slower then, in 1995, but if you worked fast, you'd be well paid for it. When Ken saw a Colorado call come in, he jumped! He thanked God she called; he thanked God he was hearing her voice on the phone.

"Shannon! Buy a map and stay where you are for twenty minutes!" He commanded. "Buy a map of Arizona! Call me back on this number in twenty minutes, got it?" "Yes," she replied. She checked her car clock and headed into the store to get the map. She gassed up the car and parked by the pay phone booth. She didn't spare Ken the abuse details; she told him too, Jay's intent to kill her. Shannon knew her brother would want to beat Jay into the ground. She didn't want that. She just wanted to get far, far away from Jay. She worried he'd go to the police and report her missing. She worried he'd have the police or state patrol tracking her down. She feared she'd have to go back to him! Ken assured her those things were not going to happen.

"How do you know that?" Shannon said nervously. Ken explained that after the two of them left for Denver, he began to trust his suspicions and doubts. He connected with his friend Craig in Phoenix. Craig worked in investigative services for a law firm, while going to law school. He did some research and found a restraining order filed against Jay. The order was placed by a woman of a previous relationship under 'domestic abuse'. That order was still in force. Ken knew Jay wouldn't be going to the police. He knew then why Jay wanted to leave the State of Ohio. Ken expected Jay would call him and he was ready for that phone call.

Ken assured Shannon, "Mom knows not to take any calls from the Denver area code." Shannon's mom was sick with worry about her daughter.

While Shannon waited the twenty minutes, Ken really went into action! He connected with Craig again in Phoenix. Craig explained Shannon would have to file a complaint in Colorado. But Ken knew Shannon wasn't going to do that. After hearing his sister on the phone, he knew what she wanted. He decided to help her go where she felt secure. Craig had an idea for that, and he too, went into action!

Ken searched the routes of truckers on the West Coast, from San Diego, then Tucson, Arizona and up to Salt Lake City. Then he checked routes, east to Denver. He tracked down a trucker heading west from Texas to Las Vegas through 'the Flag'. 'The Flag' was 'trucker talk' for the town of Flagstaff, AZ. He called their mom, assuring her, Shannon was ok.

"I've got a cargo headin' to Mile Hi through the Flag!" BJ shouted as Ken took the details down.

"What's the handle, BJ?" Ken yelled.

"Boomer!" BJ responded, "Name is Charlie James." Ken located Boomer, Charlie James, on the CD radio.

"Boomer! Boomer! Got your ears on? 10:35! 10:35!" Boomer switched his CD channel to private conversation with company headquarters. He expected to be in Flagstaff by seven p.m. He assured Ken he'd intersect with Shannon.

Ken told Shannon he'd get her to safety. He wanted Shannon to go to the police, but Shannon said, "NO!" She was running, and she wouldn't stop.

Ken kept with his plan. He arranged for Charlie to hand his sister money and any assistance Shannon may need. The trucker looked forward to being of help to the young gal, Ken's sister, on the road.

Shannon waited the twenty minutes by the pay phone and called Ken back.

"Keep heading southwest on I70!" he shouted, "I've got a trucker, Charlie, meeting you in Flagstaff, Arizona!" Ken directed her. "You've got 435 miles to go, can you make it to Flagstaff tonight? Do you have enough money for gas?"

"Yes, I've got enough for gas," Shannon said meekly.

"Shannon, you'll cross into Utah and then you'll go south to Arizona. You'll be on native American land. It's a double nickel, Shan! That means, drive 55, and slow down!" Ken's phone was ringing with calls. He noticed one of them had an Arizona area code. "Shannon, I've gotta go! I think Craig's on the line! Call me here, I'm staying late to hear from Boomer. Call me when you get to Flagstaff!"

Ken knew Shannon would feel better being out of the state of Colorado. Even though she left Jay stranded in the park she still had horrible fear. The threat he instilled in her was real and caused irrational thinking. She had trauma to her brain and body. Even though the "ex" had no car to follow her, and she was two hundred and fifty miles away from him, she still 'felt' him around her. She checked the oil in her car, studied the road map, and turned her car southwest on I70 to Arizona.

Craig heard the urgency in Ken's voicemails. What he heard made the biceps in his arms and shoulders tightened up and tingle. Hair stood up on his arms. Retaliation, fighting, was as old as history itself, and both men wanted it! Both men knew they couldn't do that. They decided to use their brains and every resource they had. They needed to stop this man in his tracks. They needed to eliminate any intention he may have of following Shannon. They planned to stop him and stop him cold.

Craig took time to check with family members in Arizona to see if he could find a place for Shannon to stay. Meanwhile, the two men devised a legal plan to give the guy in Denver a real scare. Relieved, Ken kept on working, connecting the dots, dispatching his truckers, communicating with vendors, working, working. He said a prayer, and he trusted God. He talked to Jesus. He had peace and it felt good. He remembered a Bible verse and confidence came to him, sweetly and naturally.

Proverbs 3:6 *In all thy ways, acknowledge Him and he will direct thy paths.*

Prescott, Arizona is south of Flagstaff and north of Phoenix. It's a pleasant city, with easy traffic, and a nice place to live. It was a warm day in April, and although a bit windy, the sun was shining as usual. Lena had a long list of errands to run. She was disabled from an old accident, but she could drive during the daytime. She gathered up a small bag of clothes from her closet. They were nice clothes but unusable. Her first stop of the day was the goodwill charity store drive-through. She was in line behind cars of women dropping their donations into the chute. While in line, she felt a strong intuition. She felt a voice inside her say, "*Go to Hope's Closet*." Well, no, she thought, I would have to get out of my car there, and with so much to do today... she balked at the thought of it.

The intuition came stronger; she felt and heard it again, "*Go to Hope's Closet*."

Lena knew the difference between a self-generated thought, and one of God's voice. She knew God's voice. She heard it a third time, "*Go to Hope's Closet*." When it was her turn at the drop off chute, she drove right on by it. She turned her car onto the highway. Hope's Closet was two exits down. Once there, she slipped her bag of donations over her wrist, got out her walking crutches, and entered the store. She was greeted warmly and then glanced at the lady behind the counter. It was Barb, a good friend of hers. "Lena!" Bard exclaimed, "I've been trying to find your phone number!"

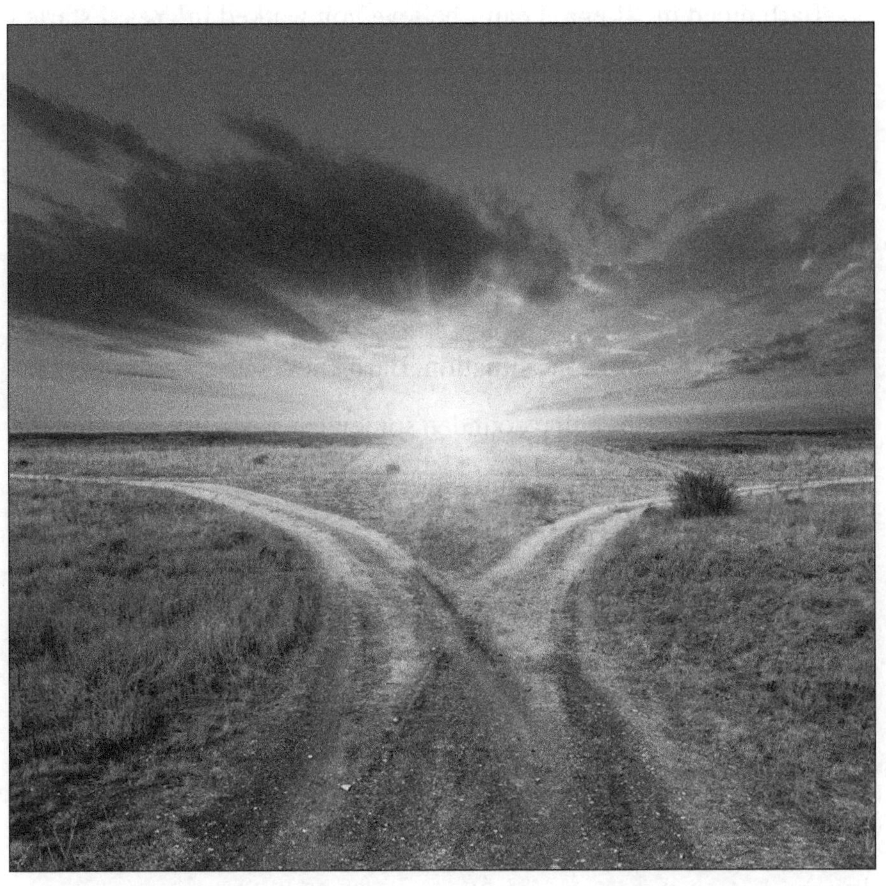

Isaiah 30:21 *And thine ears shall hear a word behind thee, saying, "This is the way, walk ye in it, when ye turn to the right hand, and when ye turn to the left.*

"Barb, when did you start working here?" Lena asked with a question on her face.

Barb piped in, "Lena, I can't believe you walked in! Yes, I started working here a month ago. Lena, you know my son, Craig, in Phoenix? He called me this morning regarding a gal that needs some help. You may remember me mentioning his friend, Ken, from years ago? Well, Ken's sister, Shannon, is on her way down from Denver."

Lena set her donations on the counter and Barb filled her in on the few details she knew of the situation. Barb knew Lena was looking for a live-in helper. Although it sounded somewhat risky, not knowing the woman driving down from Colorado, Barb and Lena decided to help. Lena agreed to allow her to stay at her home until 'she gets squared away'. Ken offered rent money and both women felt ok about things.

Barb came by Lena's house that afternoon to help her get the guest room ready. Meanwhile, Craig got the word to Ken that he'd found a place for Shannon to stay.

Shannon drove another two hundred and sixty miles across Utah, then turned south to Arizona. She arrived safely in northern Arizona. The driving was miles of empty land. She found a gas station at the Arizona border with a pay phone. She called Ken.

"Hey Sis, you're not going to Phoenix. Nope. You'll be heading to a town south of Flagstaff called, Prescott. You've got a home to live in for a while, with an elderly lady that needs some help. How does that sound?"

"Oh, wow, Ken, oh, I don't even know where I am! Yes, that sounds good, I just hope it's true." Shannon said.

"Don't worry, Shannon," Ken muttered softly. "The lady's name is Lena. She's a friend of Craig's mom. You may not remember Craig's parents, Barb and John Burnstein. They lived in Coleville and moved to Arizona a few years ago."

Shannon got back in the driver's seat, checked her map again, leaned back, and took a long breath. She was two and a half hours away from Flagstaff and would arrive early evening. She got back on the highway heading south to Flagstaff, Arizona. After Flagstaff, she'd have two more hours of driving to that town called, Prescott.

Shannon had just crossed the border from Utah to Arizona. It was a glorious moment when she saw the huge Arizona State Flag at the border crossing. It had big yellow streaks like the sun, on a bright red and blue background, with a big gold star in the center. The sign said, 'Welcome! To ARIZONA!'. A smile came across her face. She didn't know why. The flag stirred something in her. It may have been hope. If it was, it was hope for a future she didn't have a clue about.

"KB, KB, 10:5, 10:5, got a bird dog on her!" Charlie relayed to Ken. "Texaco ahead. I'll have her on radio in ten!" Charlie slowed the semi down and signaled for the turn. He matched up Shannon's car and license plate and pulled his semi into the station. Shannon knew the name of the trucking company and spotted the trucker right away. Tears of anger, relief, and pride brimmed in Ken eyes. Someone was there to give his sister support, thousands of miles away from him! Shannon had made it to Flagstaff. She was exhausted and fragile, but there was peace surrounding her, and she didn't know why.

The trucker, Charlie, was full of good-natured humor. The lights of the trucking stop made it easy to see at night. He handed Shannon some cash and a bottled water. He connected her with Ken on the CB radio. While they talked he checked her car tires and engine. He checked the windshield wipers and fluids.

Shannon thanked Charlie and they talked a bit. He had to get back on the road.

"Now young lady, I'll be in contact with Ken if you need anything."

Ken had given her directions and booked her into a safe, comfortable, and pretty hotel room in downtown Flagstaff. When she checked in, she found out her brother had paid for that, too. "Oh, Ken." She thought silently, "How lucky I am to have a family."

It was the month of April. Shannon expected it to be warm in Arizona, but it was cold! She'd seen the sign, 'elevation 8000 feet' on the side of the freeway. Realizing she only had what she was wearing, she drove to discount store. She bought a pink color, five-dollar fleece sweatshirt, on clearance, a toothbrush, and a snack for dinner. It was late, but returning to her room, she finally called her mom.

Shannon decided to spare her mom the horror of the abuse. She downplayed it to just 'verbal abuse and a shove'. She didn't want her mother to be afraid. Mostly, she didn't want her to be hurt. She didn't want her mother to have to experience what she just went through.

Shannon's mom wanted her to come home, to Ohio, but Shannon didn't want that at all. She was gone from Coleville and she had dreams. She had dreams like her brother; to do something, be somebody, and grow beyond what she'd known. She had dreams...but she'd never dreamed she'd face what had just happened.

The hotel room was cozy with a view of the snowy San Francisco Peaks.

Shannon sank into the bathtub only to discover more bruises she'd not seen before. She breathed deeply, and it shot a pain in her side. She knew he'd bruised her ribs. The pain was sharp. Another round of outrage and shock disrupted her. She didn't cry, she yelled inside her red blood cells, all the way to 'kingdom-come'. "WHY?!! Why did I allow this?!! Why didn't I see the signs?! Why did I think of marrying this person?!! What am I doing?!"

She got out of the tub. She couldn't relax. She dressed and paced the floor. She couldn't lie down. She went to her car to clean it out. She washed the windows and cleaned the inside. Her restlessness made her wish it wasn't night time. She didn't care if people thought her strange to be cleaning her car at night. She didn't want to sleep.

Then she filled up the bathroom sink and washed everything she owned. She washed her tube of lip gloss. She washed the mud off her jeans. She washed her socks and cleaned her shoes. Then she took a wash cloth and dusted the already clean hotel room. No thoughts or actions got rid of the trauma and anger. Finally, she came to a place, mentally, that made her feel a little better. The only thing that relieved her was thoughts to '*go forward*.'

Shannon awoke with the Arizona sun shining through the hotel window. Pounding of upheaval and trauma in her head, and around her head, was still there and still strong. But she was ready for the day ahead of her. She kept her focus. Something else was changing though, a new feeling, something she'd never known before. She wanted to be relieved of the trauma, the feeling of guilt, the massive horror, but it seemed things would never be the same again.

What was changing inside of her was something she felt but couldn't name. It was the formation of an iron-clad will; a fierce will power. She hadn't once felt any self-pity or the 'icky' feeling of being a victim. She felt responsible, in a vague way, for what had happened to her. She was going to make something of her life. What Shannon didn't know, was she was also creating many, 'internal stop signs'. She was saying 'no' to a future relationship with a man; saying 'no' to socializing, partying. She was saying 'no' to anything but "what would produce fruit" for her. She couldn't say 'no' to thoughts of having children; she just pushed it aside. She had much to do and children would be too far away to think about now.

Shannon learned her intuitions regarding the "ex" were accurate. He did call her brother. When Ken got the call from Jay, he read him the law. He put a shock into him. "Stay away from my sister and her family, or you'll be arrested, charged and jailed!"

Ken and Craig didn't speak fully of Shannon's ordeal to Craig's mom, Barb, and her friend, Lena. They didn't want the women to be afraid. They also didn't want Barb and Lena to think Shannon was trouble and turn away from helping her.

Both men knew Jay wouldn't know Shannon's location, over eight hundred miles away, in another state. Even so, Ken and Craig devised a plan. Craig checked with the law firm, and using legal process, he and Ken initiated a scare tactic to keep Jay from any thought of pursuing Shannon. On the day Shannon left, the police knocked on the door of the apartment in Denver, Colorado. Craig and Ken had planned well; no one ever heard from him again.

Shannon called the nice lady, Lena, before she left her hotel room that morning. Wanting to arrive at Lena's house presentably, she brushed out her hair, pulled the front of it up into a large clip, applied lip gloss, and tried to smile.

After hearing Shannon's voice and nice manners on the phone, Lena felt good about the girl. Lena went to her Bible, placed her hands on it, and with the sweetness of honey, said a faithful and loving prayer for this girl. She asked God to send an angel, to go before Shannon, and clear the path ahead of her.

<u>Psalms 91:10-12</u> *There shall no evil befall thee, neither shall any plague come nigh thy dwelling. For He shall give His angels charge over thee, to keep thee in all thy ways. They shall bear thee up in their hands, lest thou dash thy foot against a stone.*

The trip from Flagstaff to Prescott was sunny and beautiful. Shannon felt secure, knowing she had a place to go, but nothing changed with the extreme agitation around her head. It didn't pass away, and it didn't wear off. She was able to detach a little from it, viewing the world around her. The area along the freeway was lined with pine trees. She'd never thought of Arizona having pine trees and forests! As she traveled down 2,500 feet in elevation, the land turned to scrub pines and desert hills.

She passed a herd of antelope and jackrabbits in the desert as she traveled south to Prescott. Shannon felt amazed that so much had happened in such a short amount of time. Gratitude lighten her a little. Then gratitude for her brother, and everyone who helped her, increased. She said a prayer of thanks to God, even though she didn't quite know what she believed. She stopped to check her map, and by eleven a.m. that morning, Lena, welcomed Shannon into her home.

Proverbs 8:6-11 *Hear, for I will speak of excellent things; and the opening of my lips shall be right things; For my mouth shall speak truth; and wickedness is an abomination to my lips. All the words of my mouth are in righteousness; there is nothing forward or perverse in them. They are all plain to him that understandeth, and right to them that find knowledge. Receive my instruction, and not silver; and knowledge rather than choice gold, for wisdom is better than rubies, and all the things that may be desired are not to be compared to it.*

Chapter Two

Dare to Dream

Michael Coustens packed up his textbooks and notes and tossed them into the passenger seat of his truck. He hated college. He went because his dad insisted. He grabbed his truck keys, fired up the engine, and was heading happily to an installation job. He turned to exit the campus and passed a group of college girls gathered on the commons. One of them was Alexa. He pressed on the gas pedal to pass by them quickly. Funny, he thought, how she's so pretty, and full of personality, but he didn't have a shred of attraction to her. She didn't interest him anymore.

Michael's dad, Lou Coustens, owned a countertop and construction business in Prescott. He'd made a good name for himself and business was always good. Lou was a loved man. He loved God and spoke of God; he preached and taught. He knew Michael hated college. He paid for his son's college education, and he knew Michael hated that, too. "Oh, you'll thank me someday," Lou laughed, in his big, hearty laugh. He had the kind of laugh that always made people smile. "At least I think you will," he thought to himself, and laughed again.

Lou knew Michael wanted to be working, not going to school. He knew his son. He'd watched him as a three-year old with a hammer in his hand. He watched his frustrated son trying to hammer a nail at age three! The child didn't have the dexterity, yet, to do what his spirit wanted to do. Lou remembered a Saturday morning when he built a special gift for Michael. It was a peg board. He drilled holes in it, about five inches apart, with a small drill bit. The peg board was designed for Michael to be able to insert the nail in the hole and the nail would stand up. Then the boy could bang the nail down further into the hole. Lou bought a very small, lightweight hammer, just the size for Michael to handle.

Another time, when Michael was four years old, Lou heard him crying and screaming to get up on the roof with him. Lou was replacing shingles that had blown off in a storm. Michael's mom, Nancy, came out to see what the trouble was. She didn't want to say 'no' to her boy. She felt there were too many 'no's' in raising kids. She didn't spoil the kids, and if they were bad they got a spanking, but she wanted to raise them knowing they 'can do' and they 'can have'.

Nancy got out an old, large backpack. She cut holes in the bottom for Michael's legs to fit through and cut the top flap off. She placed Michael in it with his back to hers. She and Lou set up a large step ladder with a six-foot wide base. It was twelve feet high. Lou got back on the roof. Nancy climbed slowly up the ladder steps with Michael on her back. She turned and sat on the top step, facing outward. Michael could see everything from his view. Once Michael got up to the roof, and could see his dad, he stopped crying. He was happy and peaceful; he loved watching his dad.

Michael, now age twenty-three, lived in a guest house on his parent's property. They had five acres in the country. His two younger brothers lived at home. Lou thought Michael may want to run the counter-top business someday, and keep it going in his retirement. Michael didn't really want to run the business. He didn't want to just build countertops. He wanted to build alright, he wanted to work in building, but he wanted to build big! Michael's dreams were kept to himself; kept to himself, and God. A college degree may be helpful, but all Michael wanted was his full Contractor License. When he walked on campus and saw buildings going up, he was jealous of the workers! "Education doesn't teach someone how to build a building." he thought. "They don't even know how to run a nail-gun!" His drafting classes were ok, but he'd learned design and blueprints at age thirteen. He added technical courses such as plumbing and electrical, and excelled in those classes. It helped make the college years bearable. Since Michael worked fulltime, it would take him four years to get an Associate Degree. He had six months to go. With his Contractor's License on the horizon, he'd get through college; he couldn't quit now.

That night, after the installation job, Michael got ready for bed. Every night he talked to God before he went to sleep. His father had taught all the boys not to let their heads fall into the pillow without saying their prayers. He thought everyone did that. He loved that time with God. He conveyed his dreams to God and his whole chest cavity opened, along with powerful thoughts, and wide-scope consciousness.

Since he'd seen Alexa that day, he was reminded of the past. He'd fallen in love with her and had pinned his hopes on her for a future. She seemed to be everything he'd ever wanted but he really didn't know her. He was always a gentleman with her, and in his innocence, he thought he was doing what was right.

During the time he dated her, she was also dating a guy on the college football team. Michael didn't know it. He found out about it later. He found out the two of them had a close, personal relationship. But she still called him! When she called he thought there was hope for their relationship. He didn't know how to speak with her besides just loving her. He allowed her to continue hurting him. Finally, she quit calling, when Michael's friends told her that Michael knew what was up. Those nights he'd lay on his bed with pain in his heart cavity. The pain was huge. He couldn't quit thinking of her. She'd flattered him and made him feel good. She gave him attention he'd never known from a woman before. He never expected this could happen because he believed her. He loved her greatly and had been greatly fooled. Having love rejected and returned, was a bad shock. It was physically heavy on him. He didn't know how to change what he felt. He didn't know how to close the gaping wound.

When the pain reached a peak, Michael took it to God. An aunt of his once said, that the heart with a sword through it, is the closest a person will get to God. Well, he wasn't sure if that was true, but he felt God was the only way out of the pain. He asked God to take it away.

One evening, Michael put Duke, his big German Shepard dog into his truck, and headed for a trail down by the lake. He packed up a couple of Duke's favorite tennis balls, too. Duke jumped into the truck ready to go! Michael wasn't energetic. He walked up to a hilltop overlooking the water. The sky was on fire with reds, golds and magenta colors streaking from east to west. The water was quiet, and a pretty blue. He'd been noticing Duke curling up around his legs lately. Duke would tilt his head backwards, gazing up at him with big, sad, loving eyes. Michael reached out and petted him and wondered how dogs could know everyone's feelings.

Suddenly, Michael felt guilty about his dog being sad. Then humor struck him, too. He laughed at himself for caring more about his dog than that girl. He'd already asked God to heal his wound and he didn't feel he needed to ask again. Duke and he were alone in the park. People were far away. With no one to disturb him, he sat by a tree looking out at the sunset. In a moment he 'came into agreement' with God. He didn't hear a voice or words, he only knew the old, gaping wound was closing. This time, he felt the pain of it in a different way. He felt separated from it. He was watching the pain from a distance, as if he were above it, even though it was right inside of him. He simply watched the pain diminish. The gap closed, little by little, and then it was completely gone. He didn't know how much time had passed. It could have been an hour, or thirty minutes, or even ten minutes.

The sun was setting, and Duke was sitting quietly at his feet. When Michael stood up, Duke got up, too. Duke looked up at him and backed up in happy expectation. Duke backed up more, locked his legs, and barked at him! Michael laughed.

Then Michael remembered vaguely, a thought that came right before the wound in his heart closed. He thought he'd heard the words 'unequally yoked'. He didn't really know what it meant, so he didn't pay much attention to it. Regarding Alexa, he didn't "wish her well." He didn't like or dislike her. He just didn't have any feelings either way.

Michael and Duke hiked back down to the truck. Duke loved chasing the tennis ball.

That night he felt close to Jesus. He'd always talked to Him like a friend. He connected with Him and just said "thanks." He didn't ask for a new relationship. He simply asked that if he ever loved again, it would be right. With that, new confidence came, and he went on, stronger than before.

<u>Psalms 147:3</u> *He healeth the broken in heart and bindeth up their wounds.*

Chapter Three

The Council

She liked Lena's house. It was nicer than she expected. Lena, though disabled, wasn't as 'elderly' as Ken had said. Lena showed Shannon the house and yard. There was a guest house in the back yard, but it was used for storage. Lena showed her the nice bedroom prepared for her. Shannon had nothing to bring into the room. She just did the best she could. She asked questions about where to park, and what she could do to be helpful. They sat and got acquainted a little. Lena gave her some minor tasks to do.

Shannon did more work her first week than Lena asked or expected her to do. She deep cleaned the house, organized rooms, drawers and cupboards. She washed windows and polished wood. She worked outside too, in the front and back yard. She raked up the winter leaves, cleared pathways, trimmed bushes and dragged together piles of branches and debris.

Shannon loved the backyard and gardens. There were many flowering bushes along the white picket fences and patio that needed care. She tended and fertilized them.

Shannon drove Lena to a doctor visit, ran errands with her, shopped, cooked, did laundry and didn't stop working. Finally, Lena said, "Girl, take a break! Let's have a quiet time." It was a Friday night and they both enjoyed talking. They decided to make every Friday night their "talk time." Lena didn't ask Shannon about her past. She knew it was a bad situation, but she didn't interfere in any way.

Lena took Shannon around Prescott too, to see the area. Many times, they passed the Community College located centrally, in town. Lena would comment on it, and eventually she knew Shannon wanted to go to school. One time, Lena said casually, "You know a community college is thousands and thousands of dollars less than a University." Shannon shot her a look and that was all Lena needed to see.

After three weeks, Lena had no doubt God had sent this girl to her. Lena refused rent money from Ken and told him, "Shannon is a blessing!" Lena told her she could stay long term, if she wanted to. Shannon didn't earn money working for Lena, but she lived rent free, with just a few food costs.

Lena spoke in a way that caused Shannon to trust her. She'd lived over five decades of life longer than Shannon! She'd worked in the corporate world for years. She knew the power of words and importance of choice of words. When Shannon mentioned the cost of college, Lena didn't bark out, "Well, if you don't go ask you'll never know!" Lena said the words in a way that would 'go around the stopping points of the mind'. She said it this way, "If you find out what the cost is, you'll know what you need, so you can plan." Lena knew Shannon had stopping points. She noticed Shannon wouldn't talk about the cost of college for fear someone would think she was asking for help.

Lena knew too, Shannon was not yet healed of her trauma; she knew the girl was troubled. The pounding of agitation around Shannon's head was still there and the distraction was evident to Lena.

When Lena spoke of faith in Jesus, God, and Holy Spirit, she did it in her same wise way. She didn't preach. She spoke of her own relationship with God, and relayed knowledge only if asked. Sometimes though, she'd influence in amazing ways, when the situation was urgent.

On Friday night, the third week of living at Lena's home, Shannon asked Lena about talking to God. Lena was praying internally and quietly at that moment. Her eyes were shining as she sat back and allowed Holy Spirit to enter the room. She asked that this girl be set free from her torment. Shannon was feeling lost and insecure in a bewildering mystery. Lena watched her out of the corner of her eye.

Then Lena said something that Shannon had never heard before.

"Shannon, did you know, and it is written in the Bible, words of Jesus, that you are so loved, that when you were created, every hair on your head was counted?"

That night, when Shannon went to bed, she decided to talk with God. She didn't know where to begin. Lena had mentioned to talk with Him, talk with Jesus, like a friend. Shannon stretched out on her back with her hands folded over her heart. She didn't want to think anything about the "ex". She ignored the trauma of it, as if it didn't exist. She skipped it, and went on to asking God about her future, about going to college. It appeared God had other plans for the evening. His child's soul was tormented.

After a while, a thought came to Shannon she'd completely forgotten about. It came like a star. It came like an Arizona star, bright, shining and perfect in the dark blue, nightly sky. It was the memory of what the "ex" said to her when they first met. "He told me I could go to college!" Shannon yelled into the ceiling of her room.

When she closed her eyes, she saw white light around her mind, even though there were no lights shining from the street, or from lamps, or even the light of a digital clock, in her room.

"That's why I married him! Oh, my God!" she blurted out. "I've wanted to go to college all my life! Oh my God I married him for that reason!" She believed she could go to college because he said so. She married him on a strand of hope, too tiny, and unrealistic, to be true. In that hour of prayer and awakening, Shannon asked for forgiveness from God. She repented of her un-knowingness. Understanding herself, gave way to freedom. She was able to think a little clearer. Her mind lifted into conceptual thoughts. In that freedom, she forgave herself. She forgave herself for her decision to marry for the wrong reason. She forgave herself for her lack of knowing what was right. She didn't cry, but tears came. She felt God forgive her, too. Her tears were tears of stored grief; bitter and sweet, all at the same time.

Then Shannon made a deep and unstoppable commitment. She was going to go to college. She didn't know how but she was going there. She would find a way, when it seemed there was 'No Way'. She was going to make it, she'd make it on her own. She asked God to be with her and show her how.

The next morning Shannon awoke with a fully clear mind. The trauma and pounding around her head was gone. It felt so good to feel normal again, but she felt something very important had happened in the night. It wasn't about college, at least not college in this world!

While in the shower getting ready for the day, she began to recall the dream she'd had the night before. The hot water felt good. There was an open window in the shower. It allowed a warm, sweet-smelling breeze to flow in. The sounds of the water and smell of the air refreshed her. It felt so good to not be angry. She drifted off into the memory of the dream. She realized it wasn't just a dream but a vision that she'd experienced. She was shown that her trauma and anger, was far, far more powerful than she could deal with alone. She'd been forced to receive that man's rage. No one should have to endure what she'd endured. Once she was forgiven, and forgave herself, her entanglements vanished.

What was left was powerful outrage of the evil she'd faced. How could anyone treat someone that way? Her anger was pure, righteous consciousness of extraordinary power. The power of a tidal wave. No person she knew would be able to feel what she'd felt; only God. No person she knew would be able to judge correctly; only God. The magnitude of the wave lifted her far up to a place in the heavens.

She'd dreamed she met with a group of people. She remembered she was welcomed by Jesus, but then He left. The men and women were dressed in white robes and were of a supreme council. She faced them from below, at a distance, as they stood strong and beautiful above her. Then they told her to "come up here where you can see better." They told her to turn around and stand with them shoulder to shoulder. She did that. She was there to judge the debt Jay owed! She was to make the judgement! They knew she would be fair, as she was now over her own involvement. She'd experienced a great and horrible evil, and she was to respond to one part of their request. Nothing else. The union with them was a vibrational transmittance. No words were said. She transmitted to them the unrighteousness of her experience and made the decision what the debt was for him to pay. Her decision was this: *if you give fear, you must take it away*. It would be a big job for him, and not any responsibility of hers. It was a debt he'd have to pay, and it didn't matter, not in her case, if he ever paid that debt. Nothing to do with him would ever enter her life again.

The members of 'Divine Power' received Shannon's massive energy of wrongful sin against her; against love; against God. She was physically, emotionally and spiritually restored in this place of 'The Council'.

On that beautiful morning in May 1995, Shannon allowed God's energy to flow through her. She realized that no matter how, or under what reasons, a person marries, marriage is a powerful life event. She remembered Lena speaking of 'The Book of Life'. She didn't know what it was, but she thought of it as a record of all things we do in life. She'd already had the marriage annulled. She'd filed for it downtown at the Prescott courthouse. She checked the box on the form to retain her maiden name, Bradley. Still in the shower and coming back from the dream review, she announced, out loud, with happiness, "I'm Shannon Bradley!"

Then she talked to Jesus. She asked Him to erase the marriage out of her life's book. When she wrapped her towel around her, she giggled! She realized she'd also just told Jesus, "I'll buy you the eraser." Shannon had been set free.

Matthew 5:21-22 *Ye have heard that it was said by them of old time, Thou shalt not kill; and whosoever shall kill shall be in danger of the judgment: But I say unto you, That whosoever is angry with his brother without a cause shall be in danger of the judgment: and whosoever shall say to his brother, Raca, shall be in danger of the council: but whosoever shall say, Thou fool, shall be in danger of hell fire.*

Chapter Four

The Road that Ended

Shannon's eyes were filled with light getting ready for her day ahead. She opened her clothes closet and searched for something special. She was excited for her plans! She looked at the few, cute clothes she'd found at charity and discount shops. This morning she chose a pretty skirt, tank top, and shoes for the day. She felt good looking in the mirror. The tumult of agitation around her head was gone. It was gone from her face, too. She'd been working in the yard and had a summer glow. Her legs and shoulders were tan, and she liked it. Her rich color hair flowed down, long and fluffy. Ready and excited, she drove to the Community College, parked, and found her way to the admissions office.

Many heads turned seeing Shannon, tall and lovely, gliding on her way across campus. She walked into the admissions office with a smile and the sweetness of expectation. The woman at the office got up from her chair to attend her job duties. She was heavy-set with a droopy face. Her nametag read, 'Ms. McCamish, Admissions Clerk'.

Shannon said hello in a high, pitched voice.

The woman barked, "You from California?" Shannon expressed she wanted to start summer school, and said, "No, I'm from Ohio." Ms. McCamish sniffed, and said with bellicose authority, "Have you established residency in the State of Arizona?"

Shannon replied, "I don't think so, I've...I've been here about four weeks."

"Oh no, it takes a year to be a resident!" The woman said gruffly. "You have to pay out of state tuition if you want to go to school here. You can't start until you pay your tuition. Here's the cost sheet. You'll have to pay double the cost until you're a resident."

Shannon's heart began to drop into her shoes.

"You can't take all the classes you want in the summer either; they're not available. Here's the class list. Take this book too, it's a Student Guide. If you want to enroll, you have to pay by June 1st."

Trying to ignore her sinking feeling, Shannon scanned the cost of college for a resident, thinking maybe she could enroll the following year. She took the papers and the book and left. She felt like running from the building. She wanted to get away. She wondered if this was her destiny, to be broke, abused, and empty. She drove off the campus and went home. She put on tennis shoes and jeans. She walked out the backdoor and hiked up the alley behind her, to Arkin Park, on the hill. Shocked and hurt at the loss of hope, she ducked her head. The cost of college, whether a resident or not, was far, far out of her range.

Proverbs 15:13 *A merry heart maketh a cheerful countenance: but by sorrow of the heart the spirit is broken.*

Shannon walked slowly home down the park trail. Lena was gone to her women's church meeting. Shannon went to her room and rested on her bed. In a little while, the thought of feeling sorry for herself, became an irritable annoyance. She had internal stop signs for that emotion! Remembering her grandmother's teaching, she got up and said, "I'll make the best of it." In that minute, sadness retreated. She felt frustration and a little angry. "Well, at least anger has some energy in it," she laughed. She wasn't sure if she felt frustration about not enough money for college, or if she felt angry about the admissions clerk. So, she did what always worked for her, she started cleaning.

She began with dusting. She dusted the house from one end to the other. Then she cleaned the spotted kitchen windows and the glass on the front of the wall pictures. She used furniture oil and polished all the wood in the house including the picture frames. She vacuumed, straightened books and tables, did the laundry, emptied the dishwasher, and started a crock pot of food for dinner.

Lena came home to the smells of a delicious pot roast dinner, a clean house, and a live-in helper that needed some help.

After dinner they went to sit in their favorite Friday night chairs. The chairs were of the over-stuffed design, with big arm rests, in yellow and blue flowered fabric. Leaning back, with a cup of tea, Lena asked her about her day.

"You ok?" she asked.

"I don't know." Shannon laughed. Then Shannon sat straight up. Under no circumstances would she allow herself to have an attitude of helplessness. She explained to Lena she wanted to get a second job to save for college. Then Shannon told her everything, even about the hike to the park.

Lena was, of course, praying inside, as sweetly as always. She sat back and allowed Holy Spirit to enter and guide her. She began a series of questions.

She asked Shannon what the admission clerk looked like. Shannon thought maybe Lena knew her.

Lena continued, and this time she asked what the woman was wearing. Shannon could have acted like a child, rebellious, blurting out, "What difference does it make if she wore a polka dot top!" But Shannon loved and respected Lena.

Then Lena asked what the woman's height and weight were. Shannon was bewildered by Lena's questions, but she answered them patiently. Lena never failed her. Shannon quit staring at the floor and looked up to the woman who had somehow brought her a long, long way in a less than a month. Then Lena looked direct into Shannon's eyes and asked, "What were <u>you</u> wearing?"

Shannon's enlightenment came like a flash of light in her forehead. Neither Shannon or Lena said the word 'jealousy', nor did they say any words against Ms. McCamish. Words didn't have to be said. Shannon, in her youthfulness, wasn't aware of her own beauty, and she wasn't aware of her effect on others. The dynamics of human nature sprang up in the room, like water from a well. She wasn't aware too, that in her high expectations, she was a target. Shannon was a target for the miserable people in the world. It dawned on Shannon then, that she was hurt more by the actions of the admissions clerk, than the loss of hope about going to college.

Lena, in her wisdom and compassion, gave thought to the woman at the college, and whispered softly to herself, "Loneliness is extreme sadness."

Shannon detached from the situation, and regained, if ever so little, a shred of hope. That night she opened her conversation with Jesus in a challenging manner. "Jesus, you said, that if I ask, and I believe, I will receive." The room was quiet, and nothing came to her heart or mind. Some time passed. During that time, she felt urgency to go read the Student Guide. She pushed the feeling aside, but it came again.

Finally, on the third urging, Shannon got up and turned on the light. Sitting at her clean, wood desk, she opened the book. She flipped through the pages. Nothing "popped off the pages" at her. Then she got to the chapter about Out of State Tuition. She scanned the rules, and nothing was new. An asterisk dotted the last line of the paragraph. Her eyes scanned down below it. At the bottom of the page was a footer paragraph stating: 'Non-Resident students can apply for an Exemption from Out of State Tuition Fees, for the years 1995-1996, if they partake in the Campus Work-Study Program. Jobs available must meet the Work-Study qualification'.

Shannon felt a rush of energy throughout her body. Her skin tingled. Her hair tingled. She checked the calendar pinned on the wall. She looked to see how fast she'd get paid if she went to work. Next, she checked the cost of classes for the summer. Then she checked her bank account balance; she didn't have much money, but she could make it! Without tuition expenses, she'd have enough for books and classes. She'd have enough to start summer school. With a paying job, she could pay for fall semester and more. She closed the book, turned off the light and crawled into bed.

Determination solidified down deep in her guts. Along with it came her unstoppable, iron-clad will saying "Yes, I can, and yes I will." She felt uplifted, but she had uncertainty, too. She prayed again. This time she said, "Jesus, I believe, even though I don't know. Please be with me, give me faith."

The next morning Shannon pulled on a jeans skirt and an old t-shirt used for working in the garden. She slipped on sandals and headed to the college Work-Study department. The lady at the counter greeted her nicely and forthrightly, too. "There aren't as many jobs available during summer school," she said.

Shannon didn't respond.

The lady searched the big stack of data sheets, turning the pages. There were at least a hundred pages.

She explained, "Many of the jobs listed don't qualify for the program."

Shannon didn't respond.

Then the lady went back to her desk and made a phone call. She soon returned to the counter.

"The data sheets have many repeat entries."

Shannon didn't respond.

"The jobs that do qualify, during the summer months, are primarily maintenance, and not available for women."

Shannon still didn't say anything.

The lady marked something on the data sheet and went back to her desk and made another phone call. Shannon watched as she returned.

She looked up at Shannon and said, "Can you type?"

"Yes." Shannon replied.

"Can you run a computer?" she asked.

"Yes." Shannon said.

"Can you be here at 8 A.M. on week-days?"

"Yes, I can." Shannon held her breath.

"Can you be here at 8 A.M. tomorrow?" she asked, while putting the job list away. Shannon nodded 'yes'.

The lady pulled out an application and handed it to her. "Fill this out and return it here at eight tomorrow morning and I'll direct you to the training room."

The hallway out of the building looked like it was lit with fireworks! Shannon tried to contain herself. She got out to the car. She held her lips tight, but her heart was flying! She didn't drive straight home. She parked her car at Arkin Park, and hiked up the trail to the spot she loved at the top, overlooking the Arizona land and sky. A lifetime desire had come true. She wanted to tell someone! She was running up the last part of the trail. Inside she yelled, "Jesus! You're the only one who knows me! No one else will understand!"

Then humor struck her. "He already knows! But I'm going to tell Him anyway!"

This was the first time in her life she knew God was listening to her. She knew she was loved. She felt a worth she'd not known before. She got to the top of the trail, where she could see the world, and called out to Him, "*JESUS! I'M GOING TO COLLEGE!*

"You have made a way! There is a way! There is a way when there was 'No Way'! *I'M GOING TO COLLEGE!"*

<u>Luke 11:9-10</u> *And I say unto you, Ask, and it shall be given you; seek, and ye shall find; knock, and it shall be opened unto you: For every one that asketh receiveth; and he that seeketh findeth; and to him that knocketh it shall be opened.*

Chapter Five

Build the Dream

It was a Friday night and Michael sat at his drafting table. He loved imagining structures he wanted to build. He drew them on paper. This night he drew plans for an interior remodeling job he'd attained on his own. The job wouldn't start for a few months.

Michael, at 6'3 in height, good-looking, in shape, and popular, sometimes felt like a "nerdy" guy. While his friends were going to concerts, and partying, Michael was at home. One night he found himself studying car loan amortization schedules. "Wow, what a nerd I am." he thought.

His parents were financially secure, but they wouldn't be 'handing him a million' to start a project. Michael knew it would require borrowing, someday, to do what he wanted to do. So, he began research on what it would take to make his dreams come true.

Michael learned about interest rates. He saw how interest had to be paid up first before the principle was paid down. He learned what banks required in order to lend money. He studied real estate values, property comparisons, credit reports and all sorts of areas of his interest.

Finally, Michael took a business class in his last semester of college. He was 24 years old now and graduation was a month away. He excelled in the business class a bit more than he expected. He got an A- grade on an essay test and the professor commented on his "uncanny but accurate thought processes." Michael smiled, but since he was humble, he didn't pat himself on the back for the compliment. He knew work was work and college was just "for a time."

Michael didn't like truck payments and didn't owe any money. He hadn't borrowed money or opened any accounts. After his research, he knew he had to establish credit. He also knew the best thing to start with was to own his own home. He decided to talk with his dad about it.

That Sunday evening, Michael walked the three-acre trail between his guest house and the family home. He sat down with his mom and dad for dinner. He told them he wanted to 'get credit going' for the future. They had a few suggestions he decided to take. They also talked with him about buying a piece of land. Michael liked that idea! His dad said he'd co-sign, one time, for one acre of land, and take the payment out of his wages. Michael appreciated that idea, too.

Suddenly, it seemed the world had opened to him. He grinned. He knew it'd be a few years before he could start building a house, his home. The thought of just owning the land was thrilling! Lou directed Michael to get a flat lot, easy to build, and in an area of good well water. Michael felt heavenly happiness.

After dinner Michael joined Lou in his office. Lou said, "Michael, I know you're going to be very successful, and I want you to do what you want to do. Your mom and I want to travel some. With cell phones now and connection to the internet, we can travel, and still run the business from afar. I'm considering semi-retirement, not full retirement. You know our manager, Larry?"

Michael nodded. He liked Larry.

"He's stayed with us for sixteen years; the last ten, as Shop Manager. I'm thinking about promoting him to a General Manager position. You'll still be a part of the business but without any daily obligation. Michael was happy to hear this.

Lou recalled the day Larry had come in to apply for a job. He was having trouble getting hired. As soon as the business owners knew attorneys were waiting to garnish Larry's wages they wouldn't even respond to his job applications. He hadn't paid child support for a six-month period, due to a broken hand, and he was out of work. Larry sat in front of Lou and told him the story.

Lou liked Larry because he was honest. Lou picked up his phone and called the accounting department. Then he asked Larry a question.

"Are you going to church?"

Larry said 'no'.

Lou looked him in the eye. "Tell ya what, Larry. I'll hire you. The attorneys don't scare me. As soon as the wages are garnished they'll back off. It's the kids that matter. You get right with God, work hard, and there'll come a day when this is only in the past."

Larry turned out to be Lou's most valuable employee. In his ten years as Shop Manager he'd done much for the company. There were fewer complaints, fewer absences and less problems with Larry as Manager. Everyone liked him. He also increased profits for the company. He ordered and installed a dust control system in the saw shop and organized work for faster production. He worked very well with customers, too. Customers liked him. Lou decided that Larry, as General Manager, was a good decision.

Michael told his dad what he wanted to do. He wanted to start his own construction company. He'd start small and work up to bigger projects. He had the money he needed for his first materials, some advertising, and tools of his own. Michael had saved that money for a long time and he didn't need to borrow more right now. Lou understood and knew his son was going straight to the top. Lou said, "Michael, I'll take the minimum lot payment out of your check, but if you make an additional payment, whatever you can afford, you could get it paid off faster, maybe in a few years. When you own the land free and clear, it's easier to get a mortgage."

Michael would be graduating from Community College soon. He'd already applied for his General Contractor license through the State of Arizona. He took the exam and passed! He'd be working part-time for his dad, and part-time running his business. His plan was to get that lot paid for! The sooner the better. The sooner would mean he could work his own business full-time.

He walked home that night looking up at the huge Arizona stars. They hung in the sky as if they were placed there to remind people of God. He thought about some of his friends saying, "Oh, wow, dude, you have stars in your eyes!" He knew though, with God, he'd make it. He'd make it every step of the way.

The next day Michael prepared for his business. He ordered some advertising flyers, placed some ads locally, printed his own business cards, and started in. He'd take one job at a time and do it well. Value for the customer was what he knew best.

That night Lou printed the entire customer phone list from his own countertop business and handed it to Michael.

"Ah," thought Michael, "Life is grand!" He began calling customers off the list and soon had jobs lined up.

That week he called his mom. "Mom, I need some dress clothes!" Michael barked out.

Nancy loved the idea of taking Michael shopping. He seemed to have grown taller without her even noticing when! He looked so handsome as a young businessman. She wondered what he was up to.

"I've got to go to the bank, see a loan officer, and find a good accountant." He said.

Nancy enjoyed seeing her son in khakis and dress shirts. When they got home, Michael went to his house and picked up the phone. He heard his dad on the other end.

"Dad, I love you."

"Well, I love you too, son, what's going on?"

"I just called to thank you, Dad. Thank you for putting me through college." Michael said. Lou laughed with his hearty, bellowing joy.

Chapter Six

The Sparks of Summer

Lena prepared her outdoor table for a celebration. She knew Shannon would be home soon. She also knew Shannon would have good news about the Work-Study program. Lena watered the flowers around the patio table. She felt grateful to Shannon for caring for the trees, bushes and flowers. What a joyful addition to her home! Lena set out pretty, flowered English China. The teacups were very dainty. She laughed about the silliness and formality of tea service. It was a 'whimsical' contrast to holding a coffee mug. The experience would be new and add something fun to the celebration.

The patio and garden flowers were in full bloom. The roses were huge. Their colors, pink, peach and white, never looked so good. The lilacs were thriving! Lena cut some stems and made a flower arrangement for Shannon's room.

"Today is not just a celebration for Shannon's lifetime dream coming true. It's a celebration deeper than that." She said. She began to talk with God.

"Father, Shannon's traveled a road since childhood of believing there isn't a way to have what she wants. It is a road of 'No Way'. It's a road to nowhere. When 'no way' thoughts come to her now, they won't be able to stay. Those thoughts will be countered. She can no longer believe in those words! Because she turned to you, God, you've set her on a new road. She knows there is a way. Through you, she's moved a mountain of disbelief into a mountain of faith."

"And what you've done for me is just as wonderful. The faith and wisdom you've given me has been so full, I thought I'd collapse from the weight of it! This world we live in doesn't always respect older people like me. They don't value our experience and knowledge. You sent me this young lady. You sent her to me, so I would pour my gifts into her, and it's releasing me! I didn't need my crutches today! I'm walking easily with only my cane. How amazing you are. It's a delight of life to watch what you will do, and how you do it."

Shannon came home from her hike to Arkin Park. She peeked around the garage into the backyard. The look on her face was soft and peaceful. Lena smiled big. They sat at the pretty table and didn't talk much. Lena poured the tea and they both laughed.

The lilacs in the garden were thick and rich with blossoms. The lilac scent wafted over them. There were hundreds of dark violet and purple colored blossoms.

The picture of Shannon's new road came to Lena's mind. She saw it as a road for everyone. She saw it as a road above the circumstances of our lives; a road directly to God, where all things are possible.

Shannon gazed at the deep, violet colored lilacs and said, "Lena, I'm enrolling in classes tomorrow."

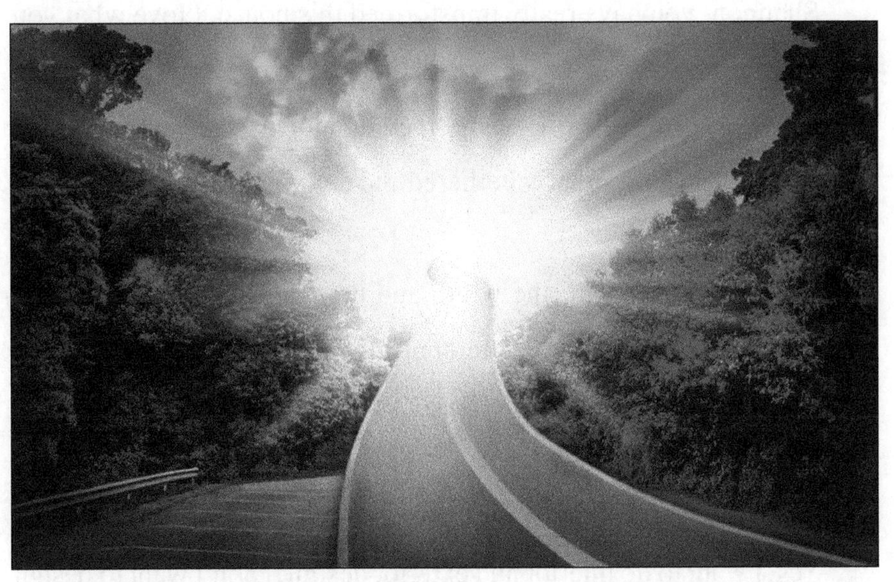

<u>Mathew 17:20</u> *And Jesus said unto them, "Because of your unbelief; for verily I say unto you, If ye have faith of a grain of mustard seed, ye shall say unto this mountain, Remove hence to yonder place; and it shall remove; and nothing shall be impossible unto you."*

That afternoon Lena's joy caused her to start talking in a cute, precious way, where her voice jumped an octave higher. It was time to go on to new things!

"Shannon, you have really transformed this house. I love what you did with the bookcases. You arranged them so whenever I look at them it brings me peace. The books are lined up and not just stuffed on the shelf. And that picture! It's bothered me for years. How did you do that?" Lena asked.

"I measured the wall; the width and height." Shannon said confidently. "Then I measured the picture frame and did the calculations. I marked where the picture should go. Now it's aligned for the space."

"Yes, it is." Lena smiled. "You have a flair for design, Shannon. Is that what you're thinking of for college courses?"

"Yes, I want to do interior and exterior design. I don't want to design with glass and steel. I'd like to do homes."

Lena smiled, "Shannon, you have done more in a month, than what I expected in a year! I've wanted to invite my church friends over, but my yard wasn't pretty. I considered hiring a landscape company, but you've done it all. You've made it beautiful. The entry way is charming, too. Do you know what I used to spend for yard work, home care, and cleaning?" she asked. Shannon hadn't thought of those things. She loved being of value to Lena. Lena was family to her.

"Here's what I want to do." Lena continued, "A friend from church, Marcy, just sold her house, and is planning to rent until she buys something else. She has her things in storage." Lena pointed to the guest house in the backyard. "It's up to you, but if you could clean out that guest house, you could live there, and Marcy can have your room. With this house in order now, and outside so beautiful, I don't need as much help as before. Marcy works full-time downtown and will pay for her rent here. For you, with two jobs and going to school, you'll need to come and go freely."

Shannon was amazed. She sat and looked at Lena.

"Lena, are you sure you don't want rent money?" Shannon asked.

"I've had this house paid for, for years." Lena replied. "The work you do, Shannon, pays for rent many times over."

Lena went on, "Now, that guest house is chucked full of storage items. We need to move them to the garage. I need to get someone to install shelves in the garage. I also need the garden gate repaired. I can find someone to do all that. Shannon, can you design the garage shelving? We need to organize it based on what's in storage."

"Yes!" Shannon grinned, "A design job! How fun! Oh, Lena, I think you are doing too much!" Shannon said.

"Darling, don't steal my blessing! I want to do this. It's a blessing to bless you, and if you refuse it, you take away my joy."

Shannon looked at her incredulously. She'd never thought of that before. She couldn't believe what she was hearing. She'd have her own place. She'd have a cottage of her own to fix up and be independent. She couldn't stop smiling.

Lena hired Molly, the daughter of one of her church friends, to come and help Shannon clean out the guest house. Lena had watched

Molly grow up over the years. She was very cute, with pretty, dark blonde hair. She had beautiful round brown eyes. Petite, at 5'5", she was slender with a lot of energy. She was going to the local Community College, too. She was friendly, social and talkative.

Lena introduced Molly to Shannon. Shannon liked her at first. But after listening to her, Shannon wasn't sure they'd be friends. Molly lived with her boyfriend and three other college students in a rental house a few streets away. Molly chatted a lot about college and other students. She'd say who was 'hooked-up' with who, and all the college life news. Shannon listened as Molly went on about this party and that party.

The two of them stacked items from the guest house onto the patio. There was much more of the guest house to clear out.

Before Molly left, she invited Shannon to a few week-end parties, but Shannon declined. Shannon explained that Friday nights were times when she and Lena talked.

"What do you guys talk about?" Molly asked with a tone in her voice. She was insulted that Shannon wasn't interested in a party.

"We talk about God." Shannon replied.

"Oh, you're one of '*those*' people." Molly said snidely.

Shannon shot her a look, and without realizing what she was saying, she said, "No, Molly, *you're* one of '*those*' people."

Molly huffed and walked out.

While the girls were working, Lena went shopping. Her legs felt better again, and walking was easier. She passed by a bulletin board at one of her favorite stores. It was full of business cards and advertisements. She read one that interested her. It said, "Small Job! Big Job! Any Job!" It had a picture of a young man, his company name and phone number.

She folded one of the flyers into her purse.

At home, at her kitchen table, she called two companies to get bids on the shelves for the garage, and gate repair. She called her son too. He lived in Seattle with his wife. He loved helping his mom, even if it was only by phone, with advice for her house.

Shannon went to bed that evening and turned her heart and mind to God. She said her prayer.

"You are our Father. Lena said you knitted us in your womb before we were born. I need your help. I feel bad. I feel bad for the comment I made to Molly. Before I knew God, I never purposely hurt anyone! I was defending my right to live my own life; the life of following you. I lashed out and it was wrong. Please show me how to be more like Lena. Show me the words I need. I want to defend my walk with you and keep from being hurt. I need to be prepared for people who think I am strange, weird, for loving you! Please Father, in your way, allow a chance for me to correct the hurt in Molly. Through Jesus name, Amen."

The following day, the young man from the flyer came out to look at the job. He impressed Lena because he wasn't wearing dusty, sloppy construction worker clothes. Lena understood the work they do; painting and demolitions. She expected the worker to look that way. But this guy wore clean, dark jeans, with a clean shirt. He had his tape measure fastened to his belt and carried a clipboard, a pen, and calculator. Lena's first impression of him was good. Her second impression was his manners and personal way of speaking. When she asked him about the cost, things were far more involved, than she'd thought. The last guy just threw out numbers on the phone, but this guy asked many questions.

"The kind of shelves to install depends on the weight of what you're storing, Lena." He said kindly. "People stack 500 pounds of weight on metal shelves meant for 150 pounds, and in a short time they have a problem."

"Oh my," Lena said. "Well, you'll have to talk with my designer."

Then she shifted herself to a playful, humorous stance, and waved her hand. He noticed her eyes were twinkling.

"You have a designer?" He asked with a smile.

"Yes, I'll arrange for her to be here. When can you come by?" Lena had made up her mind. She didn't need to compare costs. She hired him for the job. His name was Michael Coustens.

Shannon finished clearing out the guest house on her own. It was stacked with boxes and furniture. While doing that, creative ideas came to her for the garage design job. She organized the storage job with a lot of thought. She didn't want to store the books in cardboard boxes. She bought storage containers in the colors that would match the garage wall color. She unpacked and re-packed other items according to seasons and hobbies. She wrote the contents of each box on lists. Then she inserted the lists inside a clear sheet protector and taped it to the outside of the box. Shannon alphabetized each box from A to Z and wrote a master list to hang on the interior garage wall. Everything Lena would look for, she'd be able to find with ease.

Lena wanted to keep the heavy boxes of books. She scheduled a 'pick-up-junk' order for furniture and other large items. There were smaller items she decided to donate.

"Shannon, let's take these to Hope's Closet." Lena said. "I want you to meet Barb."

Shannon and Lena packed up the car trunk with small donations and headed to Hope's Closet. Barb was looking forward to finally meeting Shannon.

The three women had a lively visit.

Barb asked Shannon about her mom and brother. Shannon loved the fact that Barb knew them. She talked much more than usual. She was smiling and feeling comfortable and warm. She forgot all about her internal stop signs, her quiet, 'man-made shell'.

Shannon was not what Barb expected at all. Barb knew more, now, about Shannon's past ordeal. Her son, Craig, had filled her in on it. She expected an abused, and possibly 'subservient victim' personality. Shannon was healthy and balanced.

Barb knew Lena was doing wonders with Shannon. "One thing for sure," Barb thought, "you can't know Lena without your faith increasing."

When the women left, Barb attended to the shop. The thought of the experience of Shannon's horror came to her mind. Craig had told Barb the dangerous situation that had driven Shannon to Arizona. She looked forward to talking with her son about this beautiful and restored woman. "With God all things are possible." She said to herself. Then a favorite Bible verse came to her mind.

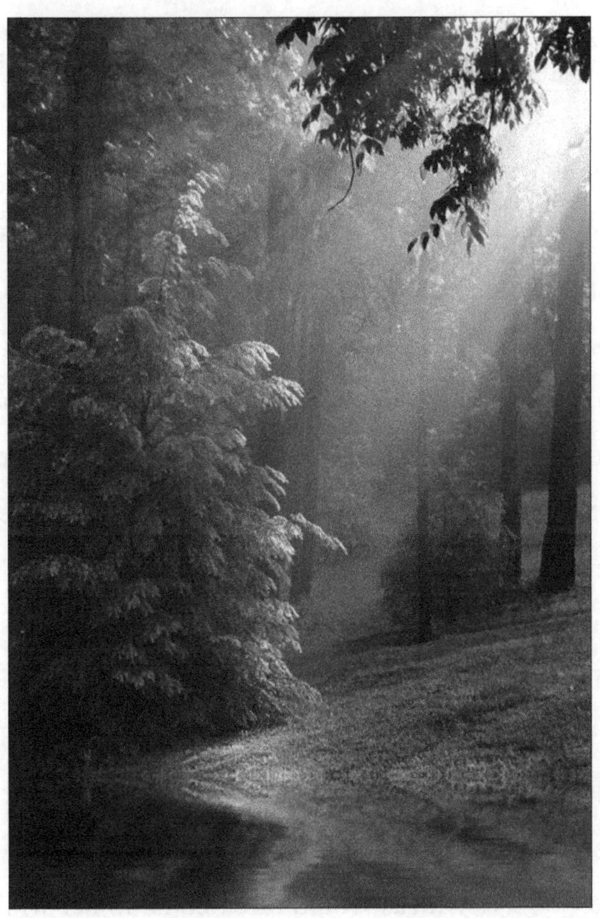

<u>Psalms 23</u> *The LORD is my shepherd; I shall not want. He maketh me to lie down in green pastures: he leadeth me beside the still water. He restoreth my soul: he leadeth me in the paths of righteousness for his name sake.*[4] *Yea, though I walk through the valley of the shadow of death, I will fear no evil: for thou art with me; thy rod and thy staff they comfort me.*

The next morning dawned in a beautiful sunrise. Phoenix was forecasting a high for the day of 115 degrees. That would make Prescott at least 100 to 105 degrees, thought Shannon. It would be 'oven hot', permeating the air and heating all structures. The sunrise blasted a rainbow of morning colors. The small hills around the area were a dark silhouette, with orange, peach and pink rays shooting into the sky.

Shannon chose a cute tank top and a short skirt she'd picked up at Hope's Closet for the day. Her legs and shoulders were glowing with a summer tan. She put on her favorite summer sandals. She pulled the front of her hair up and brushed the back out. She noticed the streaks of summer highlights in her hair. She added a tiny bit of mascara, some lip gloss, and headed to the college office.

A new stack of data sheets would be waiting for her. Her job was to enter student's names and information into a software program for college enrollees. Even though data entry was rather tedious, she enjoyed her job. New ideas would often come to her while working on the computer.

That morning she was asked to come into the manager's office. Administration had a surprise for her! She didn't work like students they'd hired before. She wasn't a 'clock watcher'. Her work was accurate. She turned in more work in half the time they expected. The manager had a suggestion for her if she wanted it. They'd assign her a college property computer to take home if she'd like to work at home. They needed office space for fall enrollment and this would free up a station area. If she agreed to return the computer, like it was when given, she could take it with her. Shannon loved the idea. She excitedly packed up the equipment and headed home.

Turning her car onto her home street she saw a big white truck in the driveway of the house. She parked along the side and decided to walk through the garage and see who was there. In a moment, less than a fraction of a second, her awareness went through the roof! The moment was so fast, it was a mini shock. Powerful attraction hit her without any warning. A handsome guy, so professional, tall and talkative, was speaking with Lena. She walked faster to get herself through the garage and out the back door. Lena stopped her. Shannon suppressed the sparks flying around herself, as best as humanly possible, as Lena insisted on introducing them at that precise moment.

It wasn't easy for Shannon to chat with him. It wasn't easy for him to chat with her either. Shannon felt every stop sign she'd ever created in her life come into full force. She acted strange, felt withdrawn, and stupid. He simply oozed with sexual attraction.

Michael Coustens handled his attraction to Shannon without anyone noticing. He wondered where this woman came from! He'd never seen her in Prescott before. He was enjoying the beauty and the fun of the moment. He felt confident with his work and managed to keep his attention on the job before him. Lena left to get everyone lemonade. It was a relief for Shannon when she came back into the garage.

"Well, have you two figured it out?" Lena asked, enjoying herself.

"Lena, do you have a scale? I think we need to weigh all the boxes!"

"Oh boy, yes, I do think I have one."

The meeting came to an end as Lena said she'd have the information to Michael by the end of the day. Michael smiled and thanked her for the lemonade. He took another look at the beautiful 'designer' and felt delighted he got this job!

Shannon walked to her new, little cottage with a 'spacey' awkwardness. She wished she hadn't chosen such a short skirt. She put the last few moments aside and began cleaning her house. Inside though, her heart felt like singing. It felt good to know she was normal. It felt good to feel that attraction feeling, even though she felt so weird!

She talked to Jesus. "That guy is so...oh...oh God, please don't let me go there!"

Lena decided to have Michael build sturdy, heavy wooden shelves. The women didn't weigh the boxes. One look at how many boxes of heavy books to store, made the decision for them.

The next day Michael set up shop in the garage. He worked smart, fast and thorough. He had the wall studs marked for shelf installation. He set up his saw-horse, nails and materials and hand-built thick wood shelving. He had a tarp across the garage floor with the shelves stacked up for painting.

"The beautiful 'designer' did well." He thought. She drew a plan for the garage side walls. The side wall shelves were open. They were narrow enough for two cars to fit into the garage. There was still room to open car doors without concern. She added lower cabinets at the back end of the garage with a countertop.

The attraction he had for Shannon was real, and constant, but he found her a bit mysterious. He took that to God. "She seems to be afraid of me." He spoke out loud. He didn't think God answered him. He didn't hear a voice, but right before falling asleep that night he knew what needed to be done. He felt a message come. The message was….'be her friend'.

Early the next morning, Shannon heard noise out of her cottage window and saw Michael repairing the garden gate. She watched him for a minute and he seemed different. Before long a knock came at her door. She knew it was him.

"Hey," he said, when she answered.

"Hey," she responded and smiled.

"Did you happen to get the shelf paint?"

"No, but I got the swatch." She hurried to show it to him.

He ignored her nervousness and said, "I've got to get some supplies at the paint store, do you want to go? We can get the paint there, too."

"Ok," she said shyly. It didn't seem she had any choice in the matter. It was her job to go but she was nervous to ride in his truck with him.

Michael knew he had to turn the flame down to low simmer. "She has some sort of a trust problem," he thought, but he didn't really care what it was.

Shannon noticed the change in his demeanor. She thought, maybe he's got a girlfriend! She didn't think he was married.

On the trip to the store, he asked her how long she'd lived in Prescott and other general, friendly questions. She relaxed a little bit.

In the paint store they accidently bumped into each other's shoulders reaching for the paint cans. Shannon didn't feel so awkward as before. They laughed, loaded up a cart, paid for the supplies, and headed back to the job.

"Turning down the flame is working." Michael thought.

Shannon picked up on it and followed suit. She seemed to be more relaxed around him.

The next day Shannon realized the job Michael was hired to do was almost finished. He said he'd be done that day. She wondered if she'd ever see him again. She'd done a good job of hiding her attraction to him; at least she thought she did.

He noticed she would 'run away' at odd moments. Whenever he started a conversation with her, she'd dart out of the room. It was that strangeness that seemed a mystery to Michael. So far, things had been easy enough. It was his job to be there, and her job to be there, so the 'asking her to go out' wasn't thought of. It wasn't his way, anyway, to ask someone to go out. He wasn't afraid of it, it just seemed too 'formal'. He wondered too, if he'd ever see her again.

That night, Michael took his concerns to God. There wasn't a response. There wasn't a response in the morning either. But on the drive home from work that day, bam! The solution came down the pike in all its brilliance! He had a job lined up for September. It seemed far off, but he could wait. It was a kitchen remodeling project where the homeowners didn't seem to know what they wanted.

One time, the homeowners chose oak wood for their cabinets, and then they switched to alder. Another time, they picked out a neutral tile for the floor and then switched to dark hardwood. Then they switched it all again and started talking about other styles.

Michael grinned from ear to ear with his new plan. He was going to keep Shannon in the loop!

Michael wanted that initial, steaming, attraction back again. He'd heard people in church say that God allows you to challenge Him. He'd never done that before. He decided to do it one night. He told God how much he wanted the original feeling back again. The desire was sweet, felt good, and was very exciting! He wanted the flame to fire up and cause her to feel the same way.

God had told him to be a friend of hers. He wasn't too sure how to do that. He wanted things to be what a relationship should be, by other people's standards. He was obeying God, but asking again, about his desire.

This time, after he prayed, he heard a voice!

This time he heard it loud and clear.

It said, "THEN WHAT?"

Michael laid back surprised. He hadn't thought it through that far.

"Yeah, if I felt that again, I'd want to take her home, no doubt about it." The room was quiet. He knew his desire had to be postponed. Michael decided to just 'stick with the plan'. He laughed, and he felt God's laugh with him.

Barb called Shannon and invited her to a dinner party at her home. Craig was coming up from Phoenix and it was going to be a fun evening. Craig was finishing law school. His parents were proud of him. Barb liked the thought of her son meeting Shannon.

Shannon looked forward to it. Barb had invited Lena too, but she had something else planned. Lena's plan was for Shannon to go on her own! The Burnstein's were like family to Shannon because they knew her family. Ken wished he could be there. Shannon's mom said to give Barb a big hug from her.

The dinner party was outside and relaxed. Shannon wore a nice summer dress. She was finally having a social life that she'd said 'no' to for a long time. It felt good not to push away good things.

Craig got Shannon's phone number and called her a few times. Shannon felt funny about it. She looked forward to Friday night, so she could talk with Lena about it.

Lena opened their conversation in a way Shannon didn't expect. Lena asked Shannon if she knew what came first, a thought, or an emotion.

Shannon didn't know.

Lena said, "Shannon, I'm not going to be around forever, so listen." Shannon didn't like hearing Lena talk about not being around, but she sat back, knowing something important was coming.

Lena went on. "The thought comes first. The thought comes first, and the emotion or feeling is a reaction to the thought. It sounds so simple, and so, well, obvious, and yet people don't know this. So, a feeling or emotion is a reaction to your thought. If the thought floods you with good feeling, then it's good. If the thought feels peculiar, funny, or doesn't have much of an effect on you, then it isn't a big deal to you. If it feels bad it is bad."

"Your age group, and even older people, warn you not to trust your emotions! But when you practice this simple system, and you put God first in all you do, then you can trust your feelings. Some people say, "be careful what you wish for, you might get it". Yes, it is true, you get what you think, whether you like it or not. The problem is wishing for something without thinking it through. So, do you see how important it is to design what you want, by creating it first, and thinking it through?"

Shannon loved the talk!

Lena asked, "So, how was the dinner party at Barb's?"

Shannon said, "You know, a guy becoming an attorney makes me feel secure."

Lena nodded in agreement to the point at hand. Shannon told her about Craig calling her. Lena knew Shannon liked Michael and she paused. Regarding Craig, she asked, "Do you like him?" Shannon got quiet. She tossed things around in her head. Lena watched her, and felt amused, in a nice way. Shannon finally said something Lena didn't expect.

"The commitment to God requires us to be honest."

"Well, yes it does." Lena responded. "But it's not just honest in our transactions."

Shannon said, "It's being honest with yourself."

Shannon looked at Lena confidently. She told her she wasn't attracted to Craig, but he made her feel secure.

Then Lena waved her hand, twinkled, and with a light-hearted tone in her voice, she said, "Oh, he'd keep you warm and dry."

Shannon smiled and mentioned to Lena she didn't know if she'd get to see Michael again. Lena sat back, knowing she was filling Shannon with things possibly beyond the girl's time to know. She asked God what He wanted her to say and got the green light to go ahead.

She looked at Shannon and said, "Shan, do you know those inscriptions written at the top of tombstones?" Shannon looked at her, bewildered again, with her abrupt change of subject. Lena continued, "The ones that say RIP, Rest in Peace?"

Shannon nodded.

"Well the heavens aren't a resting place! We are more at rest here than there. The heavens are full of energy, creativity, actions and love; it makes us look tired! What I mean is God and the heavens are forever putting people, places, and opportunities together to make our dreams come true here. Think of it like romance."

Shannon looked at her with a questioning face.

Lena went on.

"If the one that loves you knows you like red flowers, would he give you green ones? If you don't tell God what you want He gets mixed messages. Not knowing what you want is a waste of a precious life. The more you know what you want, create the details of it, and express the details to God, the more abundant life is."

Shannon listened.

Lena added, “Shannon, if you want to see Michael again, just ask, and you can be assured you will.”

Shannon read through her Fall Semester Class Directory. The college courses weren’t as difficult as she’d envisioned. So, she doubled up on them for the fall.

Her job at school allowed her to pay for classes and books and still save money. So far, she was paying her own way through college, without borrowing or receiving aid.

While doing her data entry work she noticed glitches in the computer software. It would reroute back to the wrong page, and it jumped forward on its own. It also didn’t summarize correctly. New ideas came to her of ways to make the entire enrollment system more efficient. She could ‘see’ the new system in her head. College administration could reduce a lot of tedious work with a new software program. If the entry was done once, in direct contact with the student, there would be no need for these stacks of sheets, she thought. The whole system could be reduced in time, money, printing costs and more.

She decided to visit the college computer and technology department. Even though it was summer, the department head, Dr. Meng, was working. Software programs were in demand! His department was very active and full of students.

Dr. Meng was surprised to see this pretty student walk into his office. He didn't have many women in his classes. It was 1995 and women were in the work force in droves, yet few took on computer science.

Shannon sat down and described the problem with the software. Dr. Meng listened to her because she worked directly in enrollment for the college. She knew what she was talking about.

Then she discussed her other ideas for a new system. He was impressed.

Fall enrollment was a month away! Dr. Meng put his whole staff and all his students on the project of re-vamping the entire enrollment system. The students were proud and excited to be developing a program for their own school.

Shannon was asked to do testing of the software as she knew how it should work. She did it happily. She volunteered for the testing and gave new ideas again. She didn't think of receiving credit for her work or any compensation. Dr. Meng noticed that.

Dr. Meng was highly honored by the College President for the new enrollment system. The students received their rewards in recognition and college credits. Apparently, Dr. Meng had mentioned Shannon's contributions to the project.

When the Director of Administration called her in, she wondered if she'd done something wrong. But rewarding students for extraordinary work was something the Administration enjoyed! They handed her an envelope.

Surprised and shy, Shannon opened the envelope. Inside was a document granting her six college credits for her contribution to the Computer and Technology Department and the new College Enrollment Program.

Shannon jumped. She went home to calculate her college credits. She sighed with happiness. She was on the brink of graduating with an Associate Degree in less than one year!

The annual summer thunderstorms came late, and in full force, in Prescott that year. When the ground heated up to a tipping point temperature, it pulled moisture up from the Gulf Coast. In between hot blazing sunshine were times of hot summer rain. Lightning bolts jolted vertically in the sky at night. They came one after another. They looked five hundred feet tall! They repeated fast. It looked like a million photographers flashing bulbs all at once. The clap of thunder rolled across the rooftops. Wind and icy hail blew in, right in the middle of summer! Many roofs were damaged by the wind.

On a Saturday morning, Shannon walked out to work in the garden. There were sticks, limbs and branches blown all over the yard. She was surprised to see roofing shingles strewn in the mess.

"Lena!" she called, as she entered the house.

Lena was making morning coffee. Shannon handed her a few of the shingles.

"Oooh, my." Lena said. "We'll have to get that fixed."

The next day Shannon turned onto her home street and saw Michael's truck driving away. That evening she stopped in to check on Lena. They talked about the roof. Lena didn't look at her, she just said casually, "He'll be done tomorrow."

Shannon felt a small pit in her stomach. "Oh, I'm going to miss him again!" she thought. Then she told herself to *do* something! The feeling of liking him felt good. The pressure of having to do something about it didn't.

That afternoon she talked to Jesus. She got on her knees. "I know you know me. I wanted college life, but I don't like what students do. I don't like the pressure of having to do what they do, because it's the thing to do. They all live together. They don't get married. I want to be single or married! I don't like it when they use the slang words referring to couples as 'an item' and I hate it when they talk about being 'hooked up'. I don't want that, it doesn't feel right. But I like him, and sometimes I think I love him. Of course, I want to be with him. Of course, I can just dream of loving him and pleasing him and all that comes with it. But not now! Please don't let me push love away, but please don't let it come too fast. I don't want it yet! Why do I have to like someone! I have things to do! I want things! I need things! I don't want that!"

She got up and walked around in her cute cottage. She washed a cup and saucer. She had a nice, wooden dish rack to store her plates. The plates and dishes were colorful with big flowers on them. Everything was pretty and organized in her house; it gave her peace to look at it.

While hanging up her clothes, she felt a different kind of peace come to her. She felt a powerful presence in the room; it was a female presence. She felt it very strong. She didn't hear any words. The peaceful feeling flowed over her. She felt peace that it was ok to feel the way she feels. It was ok to be who she is. Those feelings gave her freedom.

She softened and prayed again.

"Jesus, I am supposed to make my own choices. I like my friends at college. I don't want to make my choices as if their choices are bad! I like them. Their choices are right for them. Help me to not think I am right and they are wrong."

Shannon walked out of her house. The screen door slammed behind her. Lena peered out the kitchen window to see her walking strongly across the yard. Lena whispered to herself, "That's my girl."

The next day Shannon had only one early morning class, and she got the lecture notes for the class she decided to skip. Michael was at the house when she drove up. She didn't know if she should say hello or just walk on by. The old stop signs came back without warning. She wished she could just be normal and friendly, but it still got mixed up inside her.

Before she could make any decision, Michael had climbed down the ladder off the roof and was at her car window.

"Shannon, hi."

Before she could respond, he said, "Hey, I need to ask you about a design project."

Shannon lit up.

"I have some customers that need help with their kitchen remodel. I'm going out to their place this Saturday and wondering if you'd like the job."

Shannon forgot about her stop signs and said, "Yes, I'd love the job."

Then he went right on with his plan. "Well, let's get together and talk. I'll tell you more about it. What's your phone number?"

She wrote it on a notepad and handed it to him.

"Thanks" he said. "Ok, I'll call you tonight."

Shannon walked back to her guest house shaking her head. She said, "God, you amaze me every day! I was going into my weird zone. I was so happy to see Michael, and started running away from him, all at the same time. Now we are going to work together? What next?! God, what amazing thing are you going to do in my life next? I love you. I love you." A goofy smile grew across her face.

"Michael is calling me tonight." She shook her head again, happy.

Later, when the sun went behind the trees, she opened her front door and sat on the doorstep. "I'm going to work with him?" she thought. "Well, I worked with him on the shelves. It's going to be fun!"

What mattered was they were going to connect. She watched the beautiful sky turn into an exquisite sunset.

The phone rang, and Shannon's expectations were not denied.

By the end of October, Shannon had finished two design projects with Michael. The first one was working directly with the customers who didn't know what they wanted.

Shannon bought a stack of home décor magazines. Then she gathered local real estate brochures showing the styles of the area. She knew, naturally, what would look fabulous in the customer's home. She knew the dictates of their own style, too. She spent time watching their faces as they viewed picture examples. She only made soft suggestions. When they both agreed on something it was a pivotal moment. They loved her way and picked out almost to the 'tee' what she had in mind.

The second project was a home no one lived in. The owner wanted it sold. He asked for an estimate on a full exterior update. Shannon was freer to develop her own ideas on this project. She made a stunning collage display, on a cork board, for the homeowner's review. The collage had actual samples of materials to be used. She attached window frame samples, pictures of outdoor lighting fixtures, paint swatches and actual pieces of faux stone. Michael's estimate for the work was within the homeowner's budget. Michael and Shannon completed that job.

When Shannon found out the homeowner was thrilled with how his house looked, she felt the joy and value of her work. His house sold in seven days! When she got a thank-you card from the homeowners who loved their kitchen, she had fulfillment in her 'value to the world'.

She talked to God and thanked him.

"You are the only one who knows what this means to me. If I have children, they won't have the fears my mom and I had. This work isn't waitressing. I'm glad I did that. This work isn't a job at the college, either. I'm very glad I did that, too. This work is the talent you created in me. My children won't think there is "No way." Shannon giggled at that thought. "My children will be alive, without fear, like I am now. I wouldn't have found my way without you."

Working with Michael put a whole new essence into their relationship. She could talk to him now. He could talk to her. It was easy for them to be around one another. They enjoyed finding out things about each other. They shared the same enthusiasm for doing a good job, a good value for the customer. Their attraction to one another grew and expanded to more than they'd expected.

They both worked long hours and talked by phone at night.

Michael and Shannon didn't go on 'dates'. They had a friendship through their working relationship and it was fun! Respect for one another set things right.

Still, the sparks of love were there! They both knew, and hoped, there would come a time for love. When Michael asked her about being married before, Shannon just said, "Oh, I married him because he said I could go to college. It didn't work out that way." She didn't care about Michael knowing the ugly story, and he didn't want to know it anyway.

Chapter Seven

Psalms of the Heart

Shannon loved the warm Arizona winter. November was 65 degrees! She'd considered going to cold, snowy Ohio for the Christmas Holidays.

Then her mom called with news. Her grandmother had passed away. Shannon felt guilty she'd not been back to Ohio. She was sad about not saying good bye to her grandmother. They'd talked recently though, and Shannon remembered she'd told her she loved her. Shannon decided to go to Ohio for Thanksgiving and stay in Arizona for Christmas.

The thought of asking Michael to go with her crossed her mind but didn't feel right. Shannon was relieved of the thought. She knew she needed quality time with her family. Ken would be there, too. Her family hadn't seen her since she'd left there, in what seemed years ago to her. She needed to show them who she is now, today. She also needed to hear about their lives, and give them the security of her being there, in full force.

When she arrived in Coleville, Ohio, she was wonderfully surprised. Here she thought she'd be a sense of security for her mother, and she found out, her mother bought a condo! They'd rented all their lives, and now her mom was a homeowner! Shannon's grandmother, Shelly's mother, had left her an inheritance. Shelly did well investing it.

Shannon listened to her mom and a new sense of pride filled her. It was a good kind of pride. Her family wasn't poor anymore! She didn't know how to adapt to it. She still felt the overlay of her upbringing. It was what she'd identified with.

Her mom was moving into the condo in January.

Shannon's old home was the same as when she left. She walked through her old bedroom. The only thing she wanted to keep was the picture on the wall her grandmother had given her. Growing up, she'd read the words inscribed on the picture, hundreds of times. As she gazed at them today, the words came alive to her. There was an inscription at the top of the picture and a Bible scripture at the bottom.

Shannon recalled her younger years. She remembered being about twelve or thirteen and going to her girlfriend's birthday parties. A couple of her friends lived in very nice homes up on the hill. Raised on no money, she felt intimidated with their lives, and all they had. They had bedrooms decorated in all the latest trends. They could choose anything they wanted. If they wanted a bedroom all done in pop culture of the time, they got it. Shannon would shake her head. Her mom barely made enough money for food and rent. So, Shannon decided to fix her room as best she could. 'Make the best of it', was what her grandmother would say. Her uncle helped her paint her old, beat up dresser and bookcase. She chose a pretty, sage green color. Then she found a sage color patchwork quilt, with pink and pastel blue flowers. She bought it a charity store, along with the matching curtains. As important, she organized childhood dolls, trinkets and books in a beautiful way. There was a soothing design to the angles and placement of items in the room. The books were lined up that way, too. They were set up tallest down to the smallest in perfect order. She didn't like it when one book got pushed back toward the wall because it wasn't as deep as the others. So, she put rocks behind them. The spines of the books were flush and flat, right on the edge of the shelves. Her room had a 'feeling' in it, and people commented on it. Her mom called it 'cute'. Shannon wanted to tell her mom it was more than cute.

As Shannon stood in her bedroom, this day, Thanksgiving 1995, she gazed at the picture and scripture on her bedroom wall, one more time.

SHE DESIGNED A LIFE
she loved

<u>Mark 11:24</u> *Therefore I say unto you, What things soever ye desire, when ye pray, believe that ye receive them, and ye shall have them.*

Shannon didn't want to keep any of her old clothes, but she wanted her books. Her mom said she'd store them for her. Shelly asked her to sit down and talk. They sat on the edge of her old, rickety bed from high school. Shelly hugged her daughter and told her how proud she was of her and how much she loved her. Shannon loved her back. Then Shelly explained the inheritance her mom, Shannon's grandmother, had left her. She explained she'd put it into a safe, utility investment; it would pay her a monthly income. She told her daughter about a work promotion she received.

"Maaahm!" Shannon exclaimed.

Shelly had been working at the hospital part-time in inventory control. It didn't pay too well but she liked it and she had a good attitude at work. A management position came up. She told Shannon she was in this room, Shannon's bedroom, missing her, and she read the scripture words on the picture. She asked herself, "Do I believe I can get that job?" She prayed, and she believed. She also forgot about it.

Two months later, the personnel office called her in. They made her an offer to manage the inventory department. The offer included a good salary. "What is even more wonderful," Shelly said, "I love the job."

With the new condo paid in full, Shelly would be living comfortably. Shannon shook her head in amazement.

"Tomorrow Shan, we're going to see the condo, and then we're going shopping for your birthday!"

"Mom!" Shannon balked.

"Shannon, don't you think I want to buy you clothes, after all these years of not being able to give my kids anything?"

"My birthday's not till January."

Shannon stopped. She remembered Lena, and not 'stealing' someone's blessing and joy. "Okay," Shannon said. "It sounds like fun!" She giggled.

They both looked up at the picture on the wall from their heritage. Shannon still loved it. Shelly knew she wanted to have it. She said, "I'll mail it to you, honey, and I'm sending you a check, too."

Ken came home to Coleville, too, for Thanksgiving. Shannon's faith, and their mother's faith, was a delight for him to see.

On the plane trip back to Arizona, Shannon began something new in her life's path. She enjoyed the take-off and excitement of soaring upward, but emotion began to overtake her. When the unfasten-seat-belt-light went off, she sat back in her seat. She didn't expect what came next. Memories began to flood her mind, right in front of her eyes. She remembered her mom going to the store in the early morning once to get them something for breakfast. She had $1.50 and bought a box of cereal. She remembered her going to the refrigerator and nothing was in there. She remembered her mom making pancakes for dinner because that was all they had. Forgetting she was on a plane, tears began rolling down her face. She remembered Ken and herself saying to her mom, "It's okay, Mom, we love pancakes!" Tears rolled more.

She remembered her mom not wanting to work nights or weekends, so she could be with them. She remembered how many times they moved and imagined what her mom went through. The past was showing itself like a movie inside her eyes. The hardships her mom faced caused more tears to roll. She remembered her mom wanting so bad for them to have new school clothes, and they got old ones, from a charity store. It didn't matter they had old clothes. Her and Ken were happy. What mattered was her mom's sacrifices. Shannon started sobbing.

The steward and stewardess passed by with their cart and decided not to disturb this passenger at all. The man sitting next to her did the same. Shannon poured her heart out to God. In her sobs, she completely let go of all the money constriction and fear she'd known as a child. She let go of the identity she had of herself, her family, and struggles. Her mind and heart were speaking directly to God. She talked to Him in the purest of gratitude, the purest of praise.

She asked Him to forgive her for every wrong thought she'd ever had, and every sin she'd committed. Whether her sins were innocent, from unknowing, or not, she asked to be forgiven. The tears didn't stop. She gave Him thanks for her mom. Tears still rolling, she prayed, "Thank you for my mom. Thank you, for what you've done for my mom."

The Christmas Holidays came, and Michael took a few days off. He invited Shannon to go hiking. He chose a trail at a lake and Duke went too. Duke became instantly attached to Shannon and Michael loved it. They hiked quietly and steadily up a mile or so to the top of the lake.

While standing at the viewpoint he pulled her to him. She didn't resist. He kissed her and said, "Shannon, I love you."

Shannon enrolled in her third semester in college. While working on assignments she'd often visit the college library. She liked the quiet reverence in the room. She sat facing a window overlooking the courtyard. To the left of the window, on the wall, was a large State of Arizona flag. Shannon gazed at it for a minute. She remembered the glorious moment when she crossed the border into Arizona. To the right of the window was a beautiful woven tapestry. It was "The Great Seal of Arizona". The design had a miner, a hill and land, and sunrays over the top of the hill. Under the rays were the Latin words, 'Ditat Deus'. Shannon was curious what those words meant. Then she dismissed the thought. "I'll never need to know Latin!" she laughed. She went back to her studying.

The feeling of wanting to know what the words meant came again. She went to the library reference section and pulled out a Latin Dictionary. She flipped back to the section entitled 'Latin Phrases'. A, B, C… she got to the D section. Da, De, Di...she found the phrase 'Ditat Deus'. The definition was written in English next to the words. It said, Ditat Deus means "God Enriches".

Shannon's determination to get her degree was as high as ever, but she didn't want to spend years at it. She wanted to get to work in the field she loved. Her job at the college was winding down. The new enrollment system was putting her out of a job! "How funny," she thought. Administration asked her to train new employees. They granted her three college credits for it. When she calculated her credits, her heart smiled. She said, "At the end of next semester, I'll have my Associate Degree." She felt that was all she wanted. Maybe someday she'd get a Bachelor's. Her confidence level was at a place where there was no returning to the past.

Chapter Eight

Seize the Dream

Lou and Nancy took the boys to visit family for Christmas. When they got home they saw Michael some, but mainly saw him talking on the phone. Michael was busy with work and driving around with his realtor looking at lots. He called his dad on the phone to tell him about something that came up.

He took his dad to see a five-acre parcel, just reduced to a phenomenally low price. Lou liked it too. He directed Michael to get down to the City Hall and get the parcel plot plan. "Five acres for that price?" Lou said. He was concerned it may be a flood plain area or there may be a mudslide problem. He checked with Michael's realtor. He wanted Michael to run his own show, but he was co-signing. "Besides, this is a good experience for Michael to know how to check things out." He felt happy for his son.

Apparently, the man selling the property had a medical condition, and had to sell as soon as possible. The parcel was good, there were no problems, and the seller set a low price for a quick sale.

Lou spent time with Michael helping him to determine an offer. Lou taught Michael the importance of the matter and waited for his response.

"Dad, I don't want to barter." Michael said. "Most of the times, yes, you do, but in this case, I want to pay the man his asking price."

"Full offer?" Lou questioned.

"Yeah." Michael responded.

"I agree, son. It's important to make an offer that feels right to you. In this case, the asking price is more than fair. Let's put in the offer now, before it's gone."

Within twenty-four hours the offer was accepted. Michael drove out the next day to survey the five acres. He'd been there many times. Now he owned it. He could see it in a new light.

One of the acres was situated higher than the others. He dreamed he'd build his house there. Then he felt and saw a picture flash in his mind. It was instant. He knew it came from outside of himself. The picture was not 'how' to do something. The picture was what things would look like when they were done. There wasn't just one house built on the property, but eight homes! Besides his home, he saw eight other homes. He saw the houses, on one half acre of land each, and all with 'For Sale' signs in the front yards.

<u>Jeremiah 29:11</u> *For I know the plans I have for you, declares the Lord, plans to prosper you and not to harm you, plans to give you hope and a future.*

<u>Jeremiah 29:11-12</u> *For I know the thoughts that I think toward you, saith the LORD, Thoughts of peace, and not of evil, to give you an expected end. Then shall ye call upon me, and ye shall go and pray unto me, and I will hearken unto you. And ye shall seek me, and find me, when ye shall search for me with all your heart.*

Michael was dreaming and planning, for the future. It felt good. He kept at it. It kept feeling good. He'd say his nightly prayers, but he forgot to talk to God about it. The plans were far in the future. He dreamed of Shannon designing their home and picking out what she liked. He dreamed of drilling the well, and the two of them planting wind breaker trees along the property line.

He wanted to ask Shannon to marry him. There was a problem though. He kept thinking if he asked her to marry him, and told her she could go to college, he'd hear her say, "Oh, I've heard that before." He decided to take that to God.

That night, with an open and requesting mindset, he waited for direction from God. He talked to Jesus. Nothing happened. Things were quiet. No thoughts came, and he didn't get any response.

The following morning, he kept thinking of his parents. As the day wore on, he kept thinking about family. He thought about how important Shannon's family is to her. Finally, he knew what God's response was. He'd been projecting the future and ignoring today! The future will come, he thought. He knew he'd delayed in responsibility about today. Then things felt good in a real way. He re-aligned with God. He felt his feet 'flat on the ground' and his awareness strong. He felt energy and focus. He went into action!

That afternoon, Michael popped his head into his parent's home.

"Well," said his mom, Nancy, "haven't seen you much lately," she smiled. His dad walked by and hollered, "Haven't seen you in church, son."

Michael knew he'd have to go through this with them before he could speak; he hadn't been around much. "I'm going this Sunday, dad." Michael said.

"Oh yah?" his dad remarked with a grin.

"Yeah, I'm bringing a friend."

Both Lou and Nancy's ears perked up.

"Her name is Shannon." Michael announced with confidence.

Lou and Nancy were surprised! They had fun talking about it that night. Nancy said, "Michael is serious about someone? He's serious enough to bring her to church?"

She had every normal, motherly concern. First, she picked out a favorite outfit to wear for Sunday. Then every thought of 'what could be' came sweetly to her.

"Who is she?"

"What is she like?"

"Will I like her?"

"Will she be good to Michael?"

"Will she like me?"

"How wonderful to have a daughter! Will she fit in?"

Her thoughts went on and on, until finally, Lou slowed her down.

"If she's good enough for him, she'll be good enough for us, honey." Lou grounded her, and himself, too. He was happy, but he kept it low key. He knew his son was serious. This is someone special. Lou came up with an idea and called Michael back later.

They invited Michael and Shannon out to brunch after church. They chose a nice Italian restaurant by the mall. They'd leave the two younger boys at home, and order pizza for them.

Michael told Shannon the plans by phone. He had a way of not asking her, just telling her what they were doing. She loved it.

Michael was happy to have direction again; he connected with his friend, Jesus, and said, "thanks."

Shannon got out the birthday gift her mom bought her in Ohio. It was perfect for the Sunday events. She laid it out on her bed. Shelly and Shannon had a wonderful day together. They went to see the cute condo Shelly bought. They went shopping and out to lunch, too. They enjoyed life in a way they'd never done before.

Even though Shannon's mom had money to spend now, she was still conscientious about it. Shannon was glad about that. They found great deals at new stores in Coleville. Shannon picked out a soft cashmere, hunter green color sweater. The color accented her large green eyes and looked beautiful with her dark hair. She found a nice, knee-length skirt, in emerald green and black. It fit at the waist and hips and flared at the knee. She found cute black shoes in a low heel to go with it. Her mom loved how sophisticated she looked.

The morning of the Sunday plans, Shannon chose delicate, simple jewelry. When Michael picked her up he took a second look!

She was stunning!

He pulled her close and kissed her on the forehead. They held hands. Romance was sweet all around them.

As it turned out, Lou and Nancy fell right in love with Shannon! They were impressed hearing about her design work. The customers she mentioned, were people Lou and Nancy had known for years. They were customers from the list Lou had given to Michael.

After the wonderful day, Lou and Nancy came home with peace in their hearts. They could tell those two were really in love. Nancy stopped thinking of the future and wrapped her arms around her husband. They giggled together in bed that night. He tickled her and reminded her of the first day they'd met. They renewed the romantic feeling of that time. They felt they'd just met each other, once again. In fact, romance rolled over them, and love was delightful.

Shannon felt good that Michael had never initiated a sexual relationship with her. It gave her freedom, and lots of space, at a time in her life when she needed it. Had they engaged in a close, sexual relationship, it may have caused things to go in a variety of different directions. She may have felt she was repeating the past. She may have felt trapped. She may have had doubts and depression from 'too much, too soon'. She may have felt dependent. She may have walked away from him. Only God knew that!

Contrary to all the peers of their time, they didn't engage in casual or premarital sex.

Michael allowed himself to be guided by God and Shannon loved it. She trusted him. His personality was 'commanding' and Shannon loved that too! She'd gained her own self-esteem; she'd found her own security. She'd smile and laugh to herself when Michael would *tell* her what to do instead of *asking* her. She knew he'd listen to her, too. Besides, following his lead was fun! The heavens were happy because the two were "equally yoked".

> ***2 Corinthians 4:16*** *Be ye not unequally yoked together with unbelievers: for what fellowship hath righteousness with unrighteousness?*

After meeting Michael's parents, Shannon felt she knew him much better. But Michael refused to wait much longer. He wanted Shannon to be his wife. He loved her. He remembered, her birthday was coming up. That night before they got off the phone together he heard her say, "Michael? Are you still there?"

"I'm here."

"I forgot to tell you. I calculated my credits and I'm graduating in May! I want to get a Bachelors' Degree someday, but I am happy now."

The words were music to Michael's ears. He wanted her to have whatever she wanted, but possibly, just possibly, she may…she may say, 'Yes'.

"Michael, are you still there?"

"I'm here," he said softly.

"Michael, I love you."

Shannon was heading to her car on campus and ran into Molly hurrying to class. Molly seemed downhearted. Shannon spoke first.

"Molly, I apologize for the comment I made to you about '*those*' people. I didn't mean to hurt you." Shannon had been defending her right to live her own life and walk her walk with God. She didn't regret the comment she made, but she didn't mean to hurt Molly.

"Thanks Shannon. I'm sorry too for what I said. But to be honest, there's a lot more hurt going on with me right now than that." Molly said sadly.

Shannon didn't know what to say, so she remained quiet and listened. Molly didn't elaborate.

"Well, I've got to get to class." Molly said as she turned to go.

They said their good-byes, casually. Then Shannon walked about five or six feet and turned around.

"Molly!" She called to her.

Molly turned and looked.

"Come by the house sometime!"

"Okay," Molly said quietly, "Thanks, Shannon."

Michael was downtown, Prescott, at the City Hall picking up a building permit for his work. He passed by an attractive clock and jewelry gift shop. Luckily, he found a parking spot and walked into the store. The sales lady was nice. She listened well. She could read customers like a clock! Michael felt comfortable. He looked around the store, and then he told her what he was looking for. She reached up to a top shelf on the display wall and brought down a special gift. It was a gold, ornate jewelry box. It also happened to be a music box. When the lid opened, a couple skated together on the clear icy-like surface.

It played a pretty, piano song. Down at the bottom of the music box was a jewelry drawer.

Michael spent more time in the shop, until he was satisfied. When he left, he was finally, finally, happy and excited about life, in all its glory!

> ***John 4:16:*** *"And so we know and rely on the love God has for us. God is love. Whoever lives in love lives in God, and God in them."*

On January 18th, Michael took Shannon out to dinner for her birthday. He chose a restaurant with private booths. He made a reservation. The hostess sat them at a booth enclosed in polished wood walls. The only opening to the mini-room had tie-back drapes for complete privacy. They enjoyed a great birthday dinner. They also enjoyed the attention they gave to one another.

Michael handed her the beautifully wrapped birthday gift. She was very curious about it! Opening the package, she was stunned to see the jewelry-music box. Michael smiled watching her open the lid. The skaters danced together to the piano music.

Michael kept waiting.

Finally, Shannon noticed the drawer at the bottom of the box. She gently drew the drawer open. She looked up at him in amazement. In the drawer was a beautiful diamond. A diamond engagement ring.

Michael didn't a*sk* her to marry him. He told her to!

"Shannon, marry me!" he said.

There wasn't a thought in Shannon's head but what she said. She said 'Yes'.

The engagement ring dazzled in the restaurant lighting. They discussed a wedding date. Michael wanted to get married very soon, but Shannon felt they needed more time to plan the wedding.

It may have been 'God's Timing', or 'His Secret Seasons', but twenty-four hours later, the date was set for them.

Ecclesiastes 3:1 *To everything there is a season, and a purpose under heaven.*

Acts 1:7 *And He said unto them, It is not for you to know the times or seasons, which the Father hath put in His own power.*

Chapter Nine

Unto Everything There is a Season

Everyone knew Friday nights were reserved for Shannon and Lena. It'd been only a day since the exciting engagement, and a wedding was on the way, but Shannon didn't miss Friday night talks with Lena.

After her experience in Ohio, Shannon became more interested in other people. It was easier to listen and feel what they might feel. She learned more about Lena's life. She learned Lena had worked for a company that marketed business products around the world. She'd done a lot of traveling. Her loving husband died many years ago. She found out Lena's son always wanted kids, but his wife didn't. Lena had hoped for grandchildren, but she accepted things as they were.

That Friday night, Lena and Shannon got a surprise. Molly knocked on the door. She stood on the doorstep shattered and torn, very downhearted.

They welcomed her in and Shannon made hot chocolate. Molly told them her boyfriend broke up with her and went to live with another woman. On top of that, two roommates left, and no one could pay the rent. She was told she had to move out of her place.

She explained she has no money, and one month to find a place to live. Her boyfriend left because Molly got tired of partying and started going to church! Then the shocker of all hit Shannon and Lena's ears. Molly didn't cry, she just dropped in stature and said, "I just found out I'm pregnant."

Shannon went to bed that night and prayed for Molly. She prayed for Lena, too. She prayed for Michael, her mom, and her brother. She prayed for everyone she loved.

She fell into a sweet sleep. Somewhere in the night she awoke with her heart bursting with love. She had a visionary dream.

She dreamed she was running, with her heart exploding, to Jesus, in a beautiful wedding dress. Michael was in the background of her mind, strong and loving. In front of Jesus was a child. It was her son! The love she felt, exploding in her chest, was love for her son.

It was a love beyond her imagination. She felt that love as she awoke. She remembered a message that had come right before awakening. The message was …in a Season…in a Season...

That morning Shannon went quickly to see Lena. They sat down for coffee and talked about Molly. Shannon explained, "Lena, Michael wants to get married in a month! I want him to have what he wants. It would be fast-paced to get the wedding planned, but it can be done!" Then she stopped talking.

Lena sipped her coffee with her beautiful eyes shining.

"Shannon, I pondered things last night. I trust God on this, as I always do. I prayed for Molly. I prayed for God's angel to clear her path for her. I do remember praying that for you, not so long ago."

Shannon was surprised.

"Yes, if you and Michael marry in a month, Molly can take the guest house. I wouldn't mind having a little one around, too. God will bless Molly, now that she's turned to Him."

Shannon was on the phone by seven o'clock that morning. "Michael! Let's get married in a month!"

"YES!" he shouted back, "Call my mom! I'm driving to a job!"

Shannon called Nancy and then called her mom, Shelly.

Lena called Molly and then called Molly's parents.

Nancy called Shelly.

Then Nancy called the church. The Pastors wife, Natalie, called twenty other women. Immediately, plans started rolling! The wedding was going to happen…in four weeks!

The moms, Nancy and Shelly, made many phone calls to each other. Then they started emailing and calling. They went back and forth for hours in the evening until the time zone difference interrupted them.

The guest list was ready in three days! Nancy checked with Shannon and ordered pretty invitations online. The print company offered gorgeous templates, and since all they had to do was enter names and a church address, the invitations arrived by quick shipping in four days.

The guests received invitations three weeks prior to the wedding date. Shannon asked Lena if she wanted a few invitations to send out. Lena said, "Oh, I've already invited them." She had a cute smile on her face.

Shannon looked at her grinning and said, "*Who* Lena?!"

Lena smiled and said, "I've invited all the Heavenly Hosts. They told me, "Oh, we'll be there!"

Nancy made no decisions, until she checked with both Shannon and Michael, first. Although a romantic man, Michael laughed at the women and all their 'ooo-la-las'.

He finally said, "Please Mom, just do what is best for you and Shannon."

Michael was selective about his clothes though. Nancy loved taking him to the men's shop. He picked a toned-down, loose-fitting tuxedo without any satin lapels or anything shiny. He told his mom he'd wear this tuxedo if he could wear boots with it! Nancy couldn't imagine Michael in dressy wing-tips anyway. He bought nice, new black boots. It made him feel good.

What Michael and Shannon wanted most was the wedding to be romantic. They wanted it fun too, without any stiffness. The wedding would be semi-formal. The church was in the countryside and wasn't 'city-like'.

Lou and Nancy discussed the wedding expenses. Lou announced, in his usual, generous way, "We'll pay for the wedding!"

Nancy, put her hand up and spoke sweetly to him. "Lou, we can't do that."

"Nan, we've had quite a few good years. Shannon's mom is a single, working woman. We can do it. Besides, most of the guests are ours."

"Lou, that's not what I mean. Moms want to pay for their daughter's weddings. We must allow Shelly to contribute. If we don't, she may feel funny. She may feel we're acting like she can't pay. Worse, she may feel intimidated by us! It's so good of you to offer, but it may not be a blessing to her. Although people don't follow old traditions as much these days, still, the bride's family usually pays for the wedding. I'm not suggesting she pay at all. I'm suggesting we allow her to contribute a small part. I've got a plan that makes things right for both families."

Nancy showed Lou her expense list. She'd created what would look like a very expensive wedding for five thousand dollars! Shelly's portion would be five hundred dollars.

Lou looked at his wife and shook his head at her amazing ways. Nancy's wedding budget allowed for a gorgeous wedding, that no one would ever believe could be accomplished!

He said, "My Nancy, my Proverbs 31 wife."

> ***Proverbs 31:10*** *Who can find a virtuous woman? for her price is far above rubies.*

Lou acquiesced to the women in charge. He still wanted to spend money though.

The wedding wouldn't be extravagant, but it would be as beautiful as any! The reception would be held in the church. The room was huge with big windows and an updated interior. Instead of fresh flowers, silk and artificial arrangements were made by the church women. They were very authentic! Instead, of a sit-down catered reception, the church women would bring some gourmet food and some country-good food, too. They'd use their best crystal or glass bowls, placed on lace doilies, for a perfect buffet. Nancy created a fund to disperse for what was needed.

Nancy and the Pastor's wife, Natalie, enjoyed the decorating plans. The church had a storage room of wedding supplies: boxes of assorted flowers and leaves, a one-hundred-foot aisle runner, table cloths, china and glassware. There were plenty of glass vases and crafts to create any color of table centerpieces. They had music too! Taped music was available in country, pop and symphony songs.

Shannon chose pink and white, with a little bit of red, for her colors. The wedding would be three days after Valentine's Day. There would be large, wood hearts in pink and red hung on the reception room walls. Nancy and Natalie were thrilled to just keep the wall décor up after Valentine's Day.

The Church Youth Group were organized for a fun project. Nancy rented helium machines, and the kids were excited to blow up nine hundred red balloons, with ribbon trails, for the ceiling of the reception room.

Nancy didn't buy or rent chair covers for the reception. "They're beautiful," she thought, "but I'll find another way." She searched online and at fabric stores. She found three hundred yards of pink, tulle fabric, at an amazing thirty-five-cent per yard, clearance sale. The tulle fabric would be cut for chair sashes and tied with bows on the backs of the old oak chairs. She purchased some white tulle, too, for the ceremony décor.

White table cloths, pink and red napkins, white china, shiny silverware, hearts on the wall, and a ceiling of red balloons, would make the room pop with romance!

In two weeks, everything was prepared, planned and ready… everything, but Shannon's dress.

Shannon took a day off from school and drove down to Phoenix to shop for her dress. The bridal salesman was exasperated when she left the store.

"That bride looked stunning in every dress we pulled out, but she didn't like anything! She didn't like A-Line, Ballgown, Mermaid, Strapless, Chiffon, Satin, Bows, Trains or Veils!"

Shannon drove back up to Prescott frustrated. She spoke out loud to God in her car, "Jesus, help me!"

Then she knew exactly what she needed. She needed Lena.

The following day, the two of them went to a local bridal shop in Prescott. Shannon knew Lena would ease her, graciously, and help her somehow.

Shannon didn't want a plunging neckline, a low-back design, or the popular bodice style dress. She didn't want to show skin! She didn't like sexy wedding dresses. She didn't like 'simplicity' either. After declining every dress presented to her at the Prescott shop, Lena stepped in.

"Shannon. We have all day today to find the right dress. I'm taking you to lunch."

At the restaurant, Shannon was tense and unsure.

She said, "Lena, it just seems like too, too much! There are so many good things going on in my life it's hard to receive so much. Now I'm buying an expensive wedding dress. It's just...I'm happy, but...Lena, I don't know what's wrong."

While chatting, Lena knew Shannon had refused to allow her mom, or Nancy, to pay for the dress. Yet, the dresses Shannon liked were not overly expensive. They weren't out of her ability to pay for.

Lena said, "Shannon, 'Unto Everything There is a Season'. You can read that in the Bible in Ecclesiastics. You'll continue, after the wedding, to be your conscientious self, regarding 'the economy of things'. Right now, it's a season to spend and enjoy."

Lena didn't see any change in Shannon's demeanor.

Lena added, "Your mom, Shelly, and your new mom, Nancy, are in the joy of their lives putting on this wedding. They're doing that, so you can just love Michael."

With that, Lena saw a light of love in Shannon's eyes. She knew Shannon wanted to shop for her dress alone. She knew Shannon didn't want her mom or Nancy to see her uncertainty. It wasn't about the dress, but about getting married. Lena started with questions about Michael. She watched Shannon's tension drop, each time she spoke of the things she liked and loved about him.

Shannon had fun telling Lena about him. She told her about the way he talks, and the way he treats her. Shannon laughed about her own adamant nature when it comes to 'well-known-design-facts'.

"I tell him, no, Michael, you can't put river rock with stucco. You put river rock with siding."

Michael says to me, "Oh, well, there's no way you can be sure of that."

"I look at him with my hand on my hip. Before I can respond he grabs me and kisses me. We start laughing. He's so funny!"

Then Shannon really let go. She said, "I love him so much, I want to live a thousand years, just to keep loving him."

Lena enjoyed listening and didn't interrupt. She knew the pivotal moment for Shannon would come.

"Lena, I guess, I don't know.... I can't know what life will be like...I..." she trailed off.

Lena said, "Are you thinking you don't know what your job is?"

"Yes, I don't!" Shannon and Lena laughed at the funny grammar.

"Yes, I don't know what my job is!"

Lena said, "Michael's job is to make your life good. Your job is to make Michael's life good."

Lena asked Holy Spirit to show her the true source of Shannon's resistance.

Then Lena felt the wave of knowing come sweetly to her. She said, "Michael was raised with two parents who loved each other and are still married today; still in love today. You have no example of that. You are moving into Michael's home. He's known his home, his parent's good marriage and love, in his life. He has a secure 'blueprint' on love and marriage. You are entering the unknown. It takes more courage for you than it does for him to go forward."

Shannon listened and wondered about the unknown.

Lena said, "You can run away right now, Shannon."

Briefly, Shannon remembered the night she spent at the hotel room in Flagstaff. She remembered the time of running. It was running away from something bad. The only thing that felt better was to focus on '*going forward*'. That thought, again, caused something to shift inside her. She listened quietly.

Then Lena gave Shannon a gift. It was a gift of permission! It was permission to *not have to be certain*. Shannon looked at her and waited.

Lena said, "It's okay to cling to Michael until you see how fun life will be being married."

Shannon began to breathe and completely relaxed. It felt good to go forward on this adventure of life, even though she didn't know what it would be like.

"There's only one thing to remember," Lena added.

Shannon waited and looked with shining eyes at Lena.

"All you need is love."

Shannon said, "I love him like... galaxies and galaxies."

Lena smiled and said,

"Okay, are you ready?"

Shannon said, "Let's go!"

"Let's go." Lena nodded.

They left the restaurant for the bridal shop at two-thirty p.m. They checked the clock when they walked into Lena's house. It was three-fifteen p.m. In that short forty-five minutes, the perfect wedding dress was purchased, wrapped in a garment bag, loaded in the car, and they drove home.

Lena invited Shannon's mom to stay at her house for the wedding. Shelly didn't want to over-load Lena, but Lena explained that Marcy, would be out of town, and there'd be plenty of room. The wedding date was set for Saturday, February 17th, 1996.

Shelly could only stay Friday and Saturday night; she had to be back at work the following Monday.

Molly had been stopping by daily. She also joined in the Friday night talks with Lena and Shannon. Her and Shannon became good friends. Although their lifepaths, in the past, were very different, they were friends today.

Lena never judged Molly. She just loved her.

Sometimes Molly would start in lamenting about her situation. She worried about 'bringing a child into the world without a father'. She complained about her parents and their disgust with her. She worried about having to work and what she'd do.

Shannon and Lena listened but didn't lend sympathy. Finally, Molly asked Lena what she could do to help her. Lena gave Molly an assignment. "Molly, you are to go read the following passage in the Bible: ***Psalms 37:4***. Then you are to write all your thoughts about the passage and give it back to me."

Molly began that assignment right away.

The next morning, Saturday, Shannon called Molly.

"Hi Molly, what are you doing?"

"Hi Shannon, I'm working on the assignment from Lena."

"Ok, well, I'm wondering if you have time this afternoon."

"Yes, what's up, Shan?" Molly asked cheerfully.

"Molly, I have something special I want to ask you. The wedding is two weeks away. Will you be my maid of honor?"

"Shannon, I'd love to. Wow, an 'honor' is something I need. Well, in two weeks I'll only be a month pregnant. At least I won't be looking pregnant!" Molly laughed.

Shannon said, "Molly, I'm buying your dress, let's go shopping!"

Shannon and Molly found the perfect dress; a very cute, pastel pink gown. It had a beautiful off-the-shoulder design with long lace sleeves. Molly looked adorable in it!

Michael chose his younger brother, the oldest of the two, to be his groomsman.

Nancy shopped for a rose-colored dress. She found it, and it came with a rich, white and dark pink floral jacket. Shelly picked a sexy, knee-length, muted-red dress that fit at the waist, with long tight sleeves and a low back. She found it in Coleville!

Lena decided to update her looks with a hair and make-up lift. The grey color had begun to turn a beautiful white. She loved the white color and lightened it all to white. She had it cut, too, with the top of it raised up. With a new purchase of expensive make-up, her dark eyes lit up. She looked amazing!

Lena enjoyed showing Shannon what she was wearing to the wedding. She had a nice, long, dark-blue skirt. Over the top was a jacket she'd purchased years ago, on a business trip. It was hand-made in the Province of Tibet. The jacket was a beautiful cobalt blue, and navy-blue color, with swirls of gold ribbing. Inside the swirls, and all over the jacket, front and back, and down the arms, were inlaid jewels of pink sapphires, red rubies and gold topaz sprinkles.

The Friday before the wedding, Shannon was busy picking up her mom at the airport. Nancy was relieved! She wanted both Michael and Shannon to be surprised when they walked into the church. They didn't have a wedding rehearsal; Nancy had everyone knowing what they were to do. Keeping Michael and Shannon away from the church was working!

Lou left work and stopped in at the church to see the progress. When he saw what was planned for the wedding, the full impact of his son, his boy, getting married, came heavy to his heart. He wanted to do something special for them.

Before he left the church, he found Nancy in all the hullaballoo.

"Nan, where are the kids going for their honeymoon?" he asked.

"They've got a Honeymoon Suite at the Grand Canyon! They're taking a few days to hike down to the waterfall pools."

"Nan, did we invite George Nicolas to the wedding?" Lou asked.

"Yes, and he called to say he'd be here."

Lou left and went to his home office. His old friend George Nicolas, a man in his mid-seventies now, may have sold his auto dealership. He got George on the phone and explained what he wanted.

"Yep, Lou, I'm still working! Good to hear from you and I look forward to the wedding tomorrow. Come on by, Lou. I'm at the dealership. We'll find what you need, but here's a suggestion. I just got in a nice, silver, two-year old, Mercedes sedan."

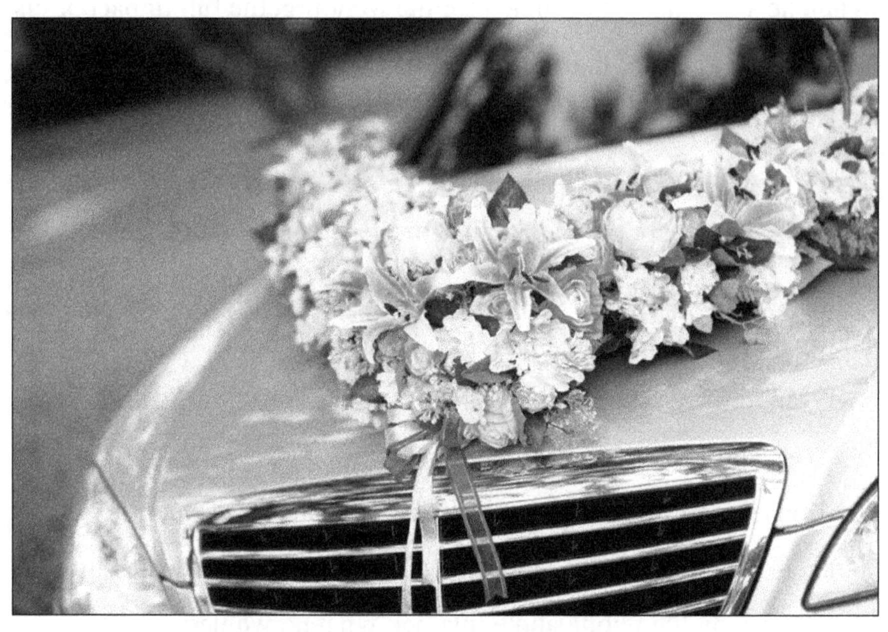

<u>Ecclesiastes 2:10</u> *And whatsoever my heart desireth I kept not from them, I withheld not my heart from any joy; for my heart rejoiced in all my labor: and this was my portion of all my labor.*

That night, Friday night before the wedding, Shannon, Shelly and Molly gathered at Lena's. While Lena and Shelly got acquainted, Shannon and Molly chatted. Shannon almost fell off her chair when she heard Molly say the words to her, "You have it all." Never in Shannon's life did she ever think a friend would say that to her! The surprise of it sunk into Shannon's mind. She reflected on her life. She'd be a college graduate in May. She had accomplishments in the work force, invaluable to her confidence. She was marrying the man, Michael, she truly loved. They were gifted with a Mercedes? The land they owned was a treasure. They'd have their house built within a few years. They'd have eight other homes to design, build, and sell. Shannon felt the truth of a Bible verse she loved. All the years of searching and it was there, written in the Bible: ***Psalms 37:4***. Shannon decided, she'd too, follow the assignment Lena had given to Molly.

Shannon knew Molly would be Lena's focus now, and the 'apple of her eye'. Shannon wouldn't be having the Friday night 'talk time' at Lena's, but she decided to go once a month or so. It would be a Friday night Michael did his drawings. That decision made Shannon happy.

The women talked into the night. Excitement was in the air; the wedding day was only a night's sleep away.

Shannon went to bed and said her prayers with a heart of fulfillment. She wished she could have a dialogue with God; a conversation! She asked that someday she would know Holy Spirit. Maybe there, she would communicate in dialogue. She told God it amazed her that people didn't believe in Him. "How can they *not* believe?" she asked.

"It's easier to believe than not to believe." She closed her prayer with thanks. She thanked God for giving her faith.

> **Matthew11:30** *For my yoke is easy and my burden is light.*

The wedding day morning dawned with excitement and activity! Nancy called early, to share with Shelly and Lena, sweet news about the wedding cake. Friends of the Coustens owned a bakery. They'd known Michael since he was a kid. They insisted, as their wedding gift to the Cousten family, they'd make the wedding cake for the cost of ingredients only. They made a three-tiered marzipan masterpiece! They'd created hundreds of pink icing flowers on the white base frosting. The top had a pretty, small gold cross, with the words written, "Forever in Love."

The wedding would start at four p.m. Nancy arranged for Michael to see the church early that morning, and the women at two p.m.

Lena's house became a whirlwind by ten a.m. Molly joined them, and all four women were fixing hair and make-up and dressing at the same time. Finally, it was time for Shannon to dawn her dress. Shelly, Molly and Lena doted on her like chicken hens. When Shannon walked out, they oohed and awed!

Shannon changed back into the outfit she'd wear to leave for their honeymoon. It was a puffy white ski jacket, green sweater, and white jeans.

"It's time to go!" Molly announced, "We have to be there at two o'clock!"

"This church! These wonderful people!" Shannon exclaimed. "Nancy, I cannot believe you did this! You and all these people did this?!" Many of the church members had known Michael for years, but they didn't know her. She'd never expected such an outpouring of love.

"Thank you, Nancy." She hugged her. Then she found her mom. "Thank you, Mom, for all you've done." Shelly was tearful and whispered to her, in her ear, when they hugged. "Shannon, I am so proud of you."

Shannon's brother Ken was happy to be her escort. He didn't have a care in the world about his sister marrying Michael. He was happy about it and acting goofy and fun. He stood outside the sanctuary door, and opened it just a little, for Shannon to peeked in before the ceremony began. Guest were listening to romantic music and waiting for the bride. There was Michael standing next to the Pastor. He stood tall, handsome, with a grin he couldn't hide. It seemed his chest was bigger. Shannon fell in love with him again! That love shone all over her face. When she stepped onto the white aisle-runner, the entry music began. The song they'd chosen for this moment was a wedding symphony of string instruments. Violins, cellos, harps, violas and piano sounds filled the church.

The congregation stood as the beautiful bride began her walk to the altar. A hush flowed over the crowd seeing her, so elegant, and so gloriously in love.

Her wedding dress was royal! The traditional, southern style dress was designed with long lace sleeves, lace covered back buttoned corset, and a full flowing skirt. The neckline was shoulder level and lightly laced. The train was just the right length; it flowed down and outward onto the floor, about two feet behind her. The soft white fabric, in silk and lace, amplified grace. It wasn't a simple dress. It was a dress for a beautiful and individual woman, of great character.

When Michael and Shannon kissed and turned to face the congregation, taking their first steps together, a giant, hooting cheer filled the room!

Then the party began!

Ken was also Master of Ceremonies at the reception. He announced Michael and Shannon's wedding dance. The crowd cheered again!

Guests lined up for the buffet but didn't sit down for long. The music sounded so good, they stood up at their tables, talking and laughing and heading to the dancefloor. Michael's old friends and some college friends attended. Molly didn't get a chance to sit down as they whirled her onto the dancefloor, song after song. Many friends of the Cousten's attended. The Burnstein's came too. Some of Shannon's friends from the computer classes were there. Craig came and was having a good time talking to Ken and Michael. He jumped too, at the chance to dance with Molly.

Shannon smiled when she saw an older gentleman walk over to introduce himself to Lena.

"Who is that talking to Lena?" Shannon asked Michael.

"That's George Nicholas, a friend of my dad's."

Shannon was glowing and flowing on her wedding day, as brides do, but she loved the romance happening with the guests, too. There was one guest she was completely surprised to see. It was Charlie! Ken had invited him and arranged for him to make it. He was on the road, and arrived late, but he 'wheeled into Prescott, Arizona'. He pulled the semi into the back field of the church and walked into the reception!

"Charlie, I'm so glad you could come to my wedding." Shannon's heart stirred. She wished she could get him a plate of food, but the women got to it before she could. Later, Ken got Shannon's attention, as he nodded to the corner of the dance floor. There was Charlie dancing with their mom, Shelly!

Michael and Shannon were so happy and beautiful, guests called it the wedding of the year!

Romance had its way. Romance had its way of bringing joy and creative thoughts about what people want for their futures. When all the people left and went home, they were in such good moods, their spirits lifted, they began to dream about their lives. They didn't go home to an ordinary house, and their ordinary lives. They went home floating, where everything seemed 'new'. They thought about their futures; what they'd love to have, what they'd love to do, and about their kids, and their kid's futures.

As for Michael and Shannon -- they didn't spend a moment thinking of the future.

Michael and Shannon loved, and rolled in love...like there was no tomorrow!

The End

About the Author:

Kathi Cousineau lives in Arizona with her husband Walter Gunther. She grew up in Washington State and received a Bachelors' Degree from Washington State University. She worked many years in the corporate world and is enjoying her longtime love of writing.

CPSIA information can be obtained
at www.ICGtesting.com
Printed in the USA
LVHW06s2340190518
577720LV00005B/15/P

9 781545 628188